Should she confess everything to her husband?

Lucie didn't want to. What would Seton think when he knew that she had deceived him like this?

But he loved her, and surely he would understand. She tossed anxiously in her bed, wondering what to do, afraid of losing the perfect happiness they shared....

Wouldn't he be appalled that he, a lawyer, had a wife who had been to prison, that his son had an ex-convict for a mother? No matter that Lucie had been innocent of any crime, that stain was on her record and always would be....

SALLY WENTWORTH was born and raised in Hertfordshire, England, where she still lives, and started writing after attending an evening class course. She is married and has one son. There is always a novel on the bedside table, but she also does craftwork, plays bridge, and is the president of a National Trust group. They go to the ballet and theater regularly and to open-air concerts in the summer. Sometimes she doesn't know how she finds the time to write!

Books by Sally Wentworth

HARLEQUIN PRESENTS

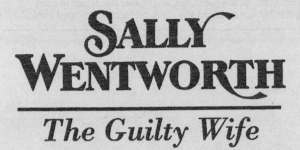

SALLY WENTWORTH

The Guilty Wife

Harlequin Books

TORONTO • NEW YORK • LONDON
AMSTERDAM • PARIS • SYDNEY • HAMBURG
STOCKHOLM • ATHENS • TOKYO • MILAN
MADRID • WARSAW • BUDAPEST • AUCKLAND

ISBN 0-373-11902-X

THE GUILTY WIFE

First North American Publication 1997.

Copyright © 1997 by Sally Wentworth.

PROLOGUE

It ALL happened so suddenly.

Lucie was cycling along the sunlit suburban avenue past the park, the trees lining the road on both sides casting dancing shadows as she rode under them. The traffic wasn't heavy, which was quite normal for a late Saturday afternoon in the small market town of Hayford where she lived. She registered the sleek-looking car coming from the opposite direction, on the side nearest the park, but took little notice, her mind occupied with her own thoughts.

Then everything seemed to happen at once. A ball flew over the park fence into the road. A big dog held by a young boy came out of the park entrance at the same moment, saw the ball and dashed after it, pulling the boy along with him.

Somebody—a woman—screamed, the shrill, terrified note cutting through the peace of the day. The car braked and swerved violently just before it reached the boy—but avoiding the boy brought it heading straight at Lucie.

The world seemed almost to stand still. The car, big and dark red, the colour of blood, hurtled down on her. Yet it was happening in slow motion too, each second long and drawn out as Lucie's mind and body became paralysed by fear. She glimpsed a man through the windscreen, his face as appalled as her own, saw him try to swing the car round yet again. There was a sickening screech of protesting tyres and brakes. And then it hit her!

The back wing of the car smashed into the front of her bike, the impact sending her flying onto the grass verge. Lucie felt herself roll over and over, her body crushing the long grass and flowers, her senses strangely aware of the scent of damp earth, of whirling sun and ground. Her arms and legs seemed to have no connection with her body, her brain had no control over them; they just flew about as she tumbled down the sloping ground, until she stopped with a jolt, her left side up against a garden fence.

She lay very still, her eyes tightly shut, her shocked brain unable to take in what had happened. Then Lucie became aware of sounds, of the woman still screaming, a dog barking, then the car engine being switched off and, a moment later, footsteps running towards her.

'Dear God!' An unsteady hand touched her neck, felt for the pulse in her throat. 'Are you all right? Can you hear me?' The voice was sharp with fear, raw with it.

Slowly, carefully, Lucie opened her eyes, and was relieved to see that the world had stopped revolving, that the sky was in its usual place. Most of it, though, was blocked out by the head of the man who leaned over her, the shocked horror clear in his eyes. She stared up at his lean face, unable to speak, and he gently brushed grass and leaves and strands of her pale gold hair from her face.

'Are you hurt? Are you in pain?'

His anxious voice, insistent on an answer, got through to her. With a tremendous effort, Lucie managed to say, 'I—I don't know.' She tried to move, felt a stabbing pain in her left arm, and promptly passed out.

She must have been unconscious for only a minute or so, because when she surfaced the man was still there, talking on a mobile phone this time. There were other people there too now. A sobbing woman clutched a young boy back against her, so closely that it must have hurt him. But the boy was staring down at Lucie, his face paper-white. Other people were gazing down at her, but the man, finishing the call, turned on them angrily, his voice a snarl, and made them step back.

Kneeling beside her again, he said, 'Don't worry. The ambulance is on its way. You're going to be fine.' Taking off his jacket, he put it under her head, lifting her only a fraction, his hands strong but infinitely gentle.

'Is that the boy?' Lucie managed. 'You didn't hit him?'

'No, he's all right.'

The woman burst out, 'I'm sorry! I'm so terribly sorry. The lead was wound round his hand; he couldn't let go.'

Lucie felt a wave of anger, but another look at the boy's ashen face made it quickly fade. She looked away, met the eyes of the car driver. They were an unusual colour, not quite grey, not quite blue, and were topped by thick dark brows that were still drawn into a frown of anxiety. 'I'd like to sit up,' she said, her voice stronger now.

'No, don't let her,' a voice put in. 'She might have broken her neck.'

'Have you broken your neck?'

'No, but I think I've broken my wrist. And I'm leaning on it. Besides, I feel like an idiot, lying here.'

The eyes lost some of their anxiety as the man, ignoring the advice being given to him from all sides, helped her to sit up. Lucie's head swam for a minute and she was quite glad to rest her head against the man's broad shoulder. Pulling his jacket round her, his arm supporting her, he said, 'What's your name?'

'Lucie. Lucie Brownlow.'

'Is there anyone I can call for you?' He glanced at her ringless hands. 'Your parents?'

'No. There's—there's only my aunt and she's away at the moment.'

'But surely—?'

He was interrupted by the wailing sound of a siren. A police car pulled up, almost as violently as the red car had done; two policemen got out and started to take control of the situation. Then an ambulance came and the man moved away as the paramedics examined her. They wanted to put her on a stretcher, but Lucie, aware of the boy still watching, insisted on getting to her feet and walked with their help towards the ambulance.

As she reached it she saw her bike still lying in the road, and gave a gasp of horror as she saw the front wheel squashed almost out of recognition. It had been a very near thing, she realised. If the driver of the car hadn't managed to swerve again it would have been she lying squashed like a pancake instead of the wheel.

The driver must have heard her horrified gasp; he turned away from the policeman he'd been talking to and came quickly over. 'I know it's a mess, but please don't worry. I'll replace it.'

Lucie raised stricken eyes to his. 'Oh, no. It's—it's not that.'

'Come along, miss. Let's get you to Casualty,' one of the paramedics urged.

'Which hospital?' the man asked him.

Lucie didn't hear the answer. She was helped into the ambulance and was glad to go, to get away from that awful scene.

It was a couple of hours later, when she'd had her arm set and was propped up in a hospital bed, that a policeman came to ask her about the accident.

When she'd described what had happened he nodded and said, 'That's the same story we've heard from the other witnesses. Mr Wallace clearly wasn't at fault.'

'Who?'

'The driver of the Jaguar. The car involved,' he explained.

'Oh, I didn't know his name. No, it definitely wasn't his fault. In fact it was his quick reaction that probably saved both the boy and myself.' A thought came to her and she said, 'Did he miss the dog as well?'

The policeman smiled as he closed his notebook. 'Yes, he even managed to miss the dog.' Getting to his feet, he said, 'Mr Wallace is still here, waiting to hear how you are. We told him you would be here overnight, but he's insisting on coming to see for himself. Is that all right?'

Lucie nodded, and as soon as he was out of sight used her right hand to try and fluff up her hair, but it had been brushed, pulled severely back and tied with an elastic band by the nurse who had washed off the dirt she'd gathered as she'd rolled across the grass verge. Her face was scratched too, and Lucie strongly

suspected she had a black eye. The hospital nightdress, washed so many times that it had faded to an
almost non-existent blue, didn't help either—not when
your eyes were the palest hazel and needed richness
of colour to enhance them. She sighed, definitely not
feeling at her best.

The policeman had pulled back the screens around
the bed so Lucie was able to see the car driver as he
came into the ward and looked round for her. He was
dark-haired and looked to be about thirty, and he was
very tall; she hadn't noticed that before, when he'd
been kneeling down beside her. He was wearing a dark
suit, the knees grass-stained, but even so you could
see that it was very well made. And he held himself
erect, like a soldier, which gave him a distinct air of
authority. The Jaguar was right for him, Lucie
realised; both were big, well-bred, and looked ex-
pensive. A lesser car wouldn't have suited him at all.

He saw her and walked quickly down the ward.
'How are you feeling now?'

'Fine.' She smiled at him. 'It was kind of you to
wait so long.'

'Nonsense,' he said brusquely. 'I was very worried
about you. I'm most dreadfully sorry that you've been
hurt.'

'But it wasn't your fault!' Lucie protested. 'It was
an accident; I told the police that. They're not going
to charge you or anything, are they?'

'No—but thanks for your support.' He smiled, the
grin transforming his face, taking the frowning anxiety
away and making him somehow look younger and
more carefree, and definitely more approachable.
Holding out his hand, he said, 'I know your name
but I haven't told you mine. It's Seton Wallace.'

Lucie put her hand in his and let him shake it; his skin was smooth and his grip strong. 'What a strange way to meet.'

'Yes.' He grinned again. 'You could say we had quite an impact on each other.'

Lucie's eyes lit with appreciative laughter but she gave a mock groan. 'That was terrible.'

'Sorry. Put it down to relief from tension.'

Because she liked his smile so much, because she was beginning to like him, Lucie said, 'I hope I'm not keeping you from your family.'

Shaking his head, Seton answered, 'No, I'm down here visiting my parents, and I've already rung to tell them what happened. But how about your family? Are you sure there isn't anyone you'd like me to contact for you?'

'No, I live alone.'

'Not even a boyfriend?'

There was a note in his voice that wasn't just polite enquiry. Lucie gave him a quick glance, her interest suddenly heightened. 'No. No one close.'

He nodded, his eyes smiling a little, but then a nurse pushing a trolley came up to them and he said, 'I'd better go. But will you let me have your address? To send your bicycle to when it's repaired,' he added, when Lucie raised her eyebrows.

'You don't have to see to that. After all, it wasn't—'

'I want to,' he interrupted firmly.

'All right. Thank you.' She gave him her address and he noted it down in a fat Filofax.

He left then and Lucie settled back against the pillows. She felt bruised all over—probably was—but also felt strangely on a high. It must be the aftermath of shock, she thought, the joy of being still alive. Or perhaps it was just the memory of a lean, good-looking face bending over her, of the width of a masculine shoulder and the strength of the arm that had held her. She might not ever see Seton again, of course; he might just send the repaired bicycle. But somehow she knew that he would bring it himself.

Her eyes drooping with sudden fatigue, Lucie fell asleep trying to work out how long it would take for the bike to be repaired.

But she saw him much sooner than she had expected. The next morning, after Lucie had dressed with the help of a nurse, reluctantly having to put on the torn and dirty clothes from the day before, she went down to the reception and asked for the number of a taxi company. But then a voice behind her said, 'Will I do instead?'

She recognised Seton's voice at once and was already smiling when she turned to face him. 'Hello.'

'Hi. You look better this morning.'

Lucie laughed. 'In that case I must have looked really ghastly yesterday. I saw myself in the mirror just now and nearly died.'

'In that case,' he said, mimicking her, 'you must look really fantastic normally.' It was a nice compliment and he looked as if he meant it. Seton put his hand under her elbow. 'The car's outside.'

He looked after her carefully, as if she were a fragile doll instead of a girl of five feet five, who weighed a hundred and fifteen pounds and worked out regularly. Lucie, who wasn't used to such tender treatment, found that she rather liked it.

She had trouble fastening the seat belt and he leaned across to do it for her. The scent of his aftershave was subtle, evocative. He was wearing casual clothes today, jeans and a sweatshirt, but the air of strong self-confidence was still there; he hadn't lost it with the suit. He drove quite slowly, careful not to jolt her around, and took a route that avoided the park, although that would have been the more direct way. It was so that she wouldn't be upset at seeing the scene of their accident, Lucie realised, and felt a lump in her throat at his thoughtfulness.

He pulled up in the road outside her flat. It was only a two-storey house converted into a flat on each floor. Nothing special. But, to Lucie, getting it had been the achievement of a great ambition, a longed-for dream.

Seton helped her out of the car and obviously expected to go up with her. Inside, he gave a small sound of pleasure as he looked around, which pleased Lucie as she'd expended a lot of loving care on the decor and furnishings.

'The kitchen is in the back.' Lucie pointed. 'Perhaps you'd like to make some coffee while I go and change?'

'Sing out if you have any difficulty and need a hand,' he called after her as she went into the bedroom.

Her eyebrows rose a little; did he expect to help her dress? But Lucie found that she could have used some help; though it was easy enough to undress, putting on a clean bra by herself was impossible. She had to give up and just pull on a loose tracksuit, easing the material over her cast. She went back into the sitting-room, where Seton was waiting. His eyes went over her, lingered for a fraction of a second too long, and she knew he'd noticed she was without a bra.

'Here's your coffee.'

'Thanks.'

Going across to the window, she sat on the deep, padded sill, unaware that the sunlight shining through lit her head like a brilliant halo. Her hair was loose now and hung thick and straight to her neck, the sun turning it into a cascade of molten gold. Glancing up, she saw that Seton had his eyes fixed on her, rapt, arrested. Lucie gave him a questioning look and he blinked, and said after a moment in a slightly unsteady voice, 'Do you work here, in Hayford?'

'Yes, in an office.'

'As a secretary? You won't be able to type with that wrist, surely?'

Lucie gave a small grimace. 'Nothing as grand as that. I just check invoices against goods, that kind of thing. I expect they'll find something for me to do.'

'But you must take some time off, give your wrist a chance to mend.' And he frowned in concern.

'I'll phone them tomorrow, tell them what's happened.'

'You promise?'

She nodded, her eyes smiling. 'I promise.' She hesitated for a moment, then, fear from past experience pricking her, felt compelled to add, 'But you really mustn't worry about me; I can take care of myself, you know.'

'You shouldn't have to,' he said brusquely. 'Look, I've taken a week off work so I'll be around. Use me. If you need to shop, go to your doctor, or back to the hospital. Anything. Just tell me and I'll be here.' He saw the surprised uncertainty in Lucie's eyes and, holding up a hand, said quickly, 'I'm insisting on this. And if you say no I shall just sit in the car outside your flat and won't go away until you agree.'

Lucie laughed. 'Are you always this autocratic?'

His eyes, more blue now than grey, crinkled into an attractive grin. 'Only with people I come close to killing.' He stood up and went to the phone, tore a sheet off the scrap pad and wrote on it. 'Here's my parents' number. Call me if you find you need anything. At any time. Promise?'

'All these promises you're demanding I make,' Lucie said on a flippant note. 'I'm not used to being made such a fuss of.'

Coming over, Seton leaned a hand against the wall and smiled down at her. 'Well, I think you'd better start getting used to it.' She didn't speak and he walked to the door, then turned. 'You won't want to cook tonight; how about sharing a Chinese take away?'

Lucie hesitated, knew that she ought to refuse, but found herself saying, 'I'd like that.'

He let himself out and Lucie watched from the window as he left, lifting a hand to wave to her before he got in the car. She watched him go with mixed feelings. He was a very attractive man, not the kind she came across very often. A man it would be easy to fall for. There was something about him that had got to her, and from the way he'd looked at her once or twice she thought that he might feel the same about her.

The thought excited Lucie but made her nervous, too. She hadn't much experience of men, and what she had was all bad. But probably she was wrong; Seton was most likely just being kind, and once his week's holiday was over and her wrist improved she would never see him again.

It didn't work out like that. Her heart gave a jolt the minute she opened the door to him that evening and saw his smile again. Immediately she felt happy, excited, as if something wonderful was about to happen.

They sat long over their meal, talking in a relaxed, comfortable way, not as virtual strangers but as if they'd known each other for ages. It was Seton's ease of manner, his ability to start and hold so many topics, and the way he subtly drew her out to talk about herself that made it so comfortable.

Lucie responded with more enjoyment and animation than she'd known for years, perhaps had ever known. She told him a great deal about herself, of the Open University course she was taking and her hopes for the future. But she didn't tell him everything, glossing over her past and quickly bringing the subject back to him. In turn Seton told her of his love of sport and travel, then totally disconcerted her by saying that he was a practising barrister.

Thankfully, Seton was refilling their glasses and didn't notice the effect that piece of information had on her. Lucie was struck by how strange it was that she should be here with him. A barrister, of all things! And he was so much more polished than anyone she'd met before, so socially confident and assured. She couldn't imagine him ever being unable to handle a situation. And it wasn't an acquired confidence but something that had been bred into him, a kind of arrogance, if a profound belief in the principles and values handed down to one could be called arrogance. He was, to put it bluntly, in a class light years from her own.

That knowledge, and the fact that he was a barrister, ought to have put her off, or at least have acted as a warning, but his attraction was too great for her to heed it. Lucie liked the way he continued to look after her, and she liked the way the candlelight cast shadows on his face, accentuating the leanness of his high cheekbones, the fan of his eyelashes and the laughter lines around his mouth when he smiled. He had a good voice, deep, well modulated, educated but not over the top, and he knew how to tell an anecdote to get the best out of it, to make her laugh richly.

When the evening was over, when Seton could find no excuse to linger any longer, he moved reluctantly towards the door and said, 'You're quite sure there's nothing else I can do?'

'Quite sure. You've already been kind beyond the call of conscience.'

She was standing near the front door, waiting for him, her fair hair a silken sheen in the light of the lamps she'd lit. Coming close, Seton said softly, 'If you think that's the only reason I came, you couldn't be more wrong.'

Lucie was aware of his closeness, of his masculinity, and for a moment became nervous again. Holding out her right hand, she said with formal politeness, 'Goodnight, Seton. Thank you for the meal.'

He looked at her, then disconcerted her again by taking her hand and raising it fleetingly to his lips. 'Goodnight, Lucie.'

Closing the door behind him, Lucie leaned against the wall, feeling enchanted by that unexpected gesture and yet strangely low now that he had gone. For a while she had felt feminine and pretty and—cherished: a sensation that had never come her way before. But she had liked it, oh, *how* she had liked it. And how she had likcd him.

She went to move away, but there was a sharp double knock on the door panel, just near her head. Slowly Lucie reached out and turned the knob, let the door swing open. Seton was standing there, one arm up against the doorframe. He said, 'I forgot to ask. Do you believe in kissing on a first date?'

'No, definitely not.'

'Nor do I.' Coming inside, he shouldered the door closed. 'In that case, we'd better call this our second date.' And, taking her in his arms, he drew her to him and kissed her.

When Seton raised his head at last, Lucie kept her eyes tight closed, afraid of breaking the spell. Because it couldn't be true, it couldn't be real. No kiss, no simple coming together of a man's and a woman's mouth, could possibly be that wonderful. She lived it again: the sensual warmth of his lips, the dizzying effect on her senses, the discovery deep inside her of awakened need—a need that could so easily have flamed into fierce passion and desire.

'Hey,' he said softly against her mouth. 'Have you gone to sleep?'

Still with her eyes closed, Lucie smiled. 'No, but I think I'm dreaming.'

'Is that good or bad?'

She looked at him, then said huskily, 'Oh, it was very good. Do you always have that effect on the women you kiss?'

'What effect?'

Slowly she reached up to touch his face, letting her fingers trace the line of his jaw. 'Devastating,' she admitted honestly.

He gave a sigh of satisfaction and pleasure. 'Thank God for that! It would have been terrible if it had all been one-sided.'

Her eyes widened. 'You—you mean it was like that for you too?'

'Of course.' Seton grinned. 'But perhaps we should do it again and make sure.'

It was what Lucie wanted more than anything else in the world, but some note of caution made her say, 'This—you... It's all happening so fast. I don't *know* you.'

Seton laughed. 'Well, I don't know you either, but I'm willing to take a chance.' Her face changed, became stricken, and he said quickly, 'Lucie! What is it? I was only joking.'

'Yes—but you *don't* know me.'

'So we'll get to know each other. We'll do that old-fashioned thing they used to call courting. We will go out together, and we'll take our time.'

'And—and this?'

Realising what she meant, he held her closer and said softly, 'I won't rush you into anything. I'll let you set the pace. But I would like to kiss you again. Now. May I?'

But he didn't wait for her to agree; his hands were already cupping her face, tilting her head so that his lips could seek hers, so lightly at first, softly exploring, tracing with tiny kisses the length of her upper lip, gently biting at the fullness of the lower one. Then, using the tip of his tongue, he made her open her mouth and let him in, and suddenly his lips weren't gentle any more, but hot and forceful and demanding.

Lucie gave a small moan and closed her eyes, letting him take her with him on a deep spiral of pleasure, where the world was lost and the only sensations were those of his closeness, of the flame of passion that erupted through her veins—the need, the desire, the knowledge that for her nothing in the world had ever been as wonderful as this, that nothing else mattered so much.

Seton's shoulders hunched as he kissed her, his breathing quickened and he said her name over and over again, his voice thick, the murmured name mingling with her own gasping sighs. His kiss deepened with passion until he drew back suddenly, remembering his promise. Lifting his head, he held her against his chest and she could feel the beating of his heart.

'I'm afraid,' she said, with an honesty he couldn't possibly understand.

'I know, but there's no need to be, my darling. I'll take care of you.'

'Please—I think you'd better go now.'

'You don't trust me, huh?' He smiled tenderly down at her. 'Well, maybe you're right; I've never found myself in this kind of situation before.'

'What kind?'

His eyes crinkled and he gave her lips the merest touch with his. 'Wild about you, of course.' And then he opened the door and was gone as Lucie still stood with eyes open wide in astonishment.

Seton came to collect her the next morning, buoyant, on a high, reaching out to kiss her as soon as he arrived. Lucie, too, was exhilarated by excitement, but was also full of nervous tension. She could see happiness opening before her but was afraid to grasp it, so she held him off.

'No! Don't touch me,' she cried out, knowing that she would be lost if he held her.

But he put his hands on her shoulders and said, 'Lucie? What is it?'

'This—this attraction you feel. It could be just a chemical thing, something that's hit us out of the blue.'

'Ah, so you admit it hit you too,' he said with satisfaction.

Ignoring that, Lucie said, 'How do you know it won't go away as suddenly as it came? You might wake up one morning and hate the sight of me.'

'If I woke up with you beside me it couldn't be anything but wonderful—perfect,' Seton said simply.

She tried to argue with him, to point out that something that had happened so quickly couldn't possibly last. But Seton merely laughed and pulled her into his arms.

Lucie gave a sigh of frustration. 'Oh, you big fool! Why won't you listen to me? Take me seriously?'

But then he kissed her and immediately Lucie was lost again, and somehow she knew that she always would be, that whenever he kissed her it would always be like this, a total domination of her mind, her heart and her body. And yet she accepted it gladly, glorying in it, knowing that it was the same for him.

He was, she observed, unchangeable, and he proved it in the next weeks as he saw her as often as he could. That first week he was around all the time, driving her wherever she wanted to go, taking her out to eat, solicitous about her injured wrist. And after the first week, when he had to go back to London to work, he put a great many miles on the Jaguar as he drove down to take her to dinner and the theatre—places that she would never have gone to normally. He didn't seem at all short of money, and although he didn't throw it around he was always very generous, booking the best seats at the theatre or cinema, tables at well-known restaurants.

Although he obeyed the rules she'd set down for them to get to know each other better and not to rush things, Seton was quite capable of trying to break down her defences. Often, when they said goodnight, he would kiss her so passionately that it almost broke her resolve, but somehow she managed to push him away, to send him home empty and unfulfilled, as frustrated as she was herself.

It was a long, hot summer, and one day, when they'd known each other about six weeks, Seton hired a boat for the day and rowed her down the river that meandered through the old town, making sure she had cushions to make her comfortable, although her wrist was almost mended now. He'd brought a picnic hamper and dangled a bottle of wine over the side to keep it cool until they came to a quiet spot of trees and dappled sunlight. There Seton moored and helped her onto the bank.

He laid a rug down on the grass and they ate and drank, listening to old, trad jazz tunes on a cassette player. He had taken off his shirt because of the heat and, although she tried to resist, Lucie found her eyes drawn to his broad, smooth chest and the muscles that rippled in his shoulders and arms. The slight breeze made the leaves above them move, casting shadows that played across his body, first high-lighting a shoulder, then the tiny, fascinating nipples, then the length of his back as he turned away from her to repack the hamper.

It was erotic, sexy, as if some mischievous Cupid had deliberately set out to tease and tantalise her senses. Lucie's throat tightened and she felt a fierce surge of longing, an emotion so strong that almost of its own volition her hand lifted and she touched his back, letting her fingers trail down the length of his spine. She felt a great quiver of awareness run through him before Seton turned swiftly to face her. The need for her was there in his eyes—deep, intense concupiscence. A need, she knew, that was mirrored in her own.

'Lucie.' He said her name on a long, low breath of discovery and pleasure. Reaching out a trembling, unsteady hand, he put it on her cheek and slowly stroked her face, holding her eyes all the time. Then he came up on his knees so that he could bend to kiss her.

His lips were hot, eager, quivering with anticipation. Putting her hand on his shoulder, Lucie felt his skin taut and damp with perspiration, not from the heat but from the excitement of knowing that she wanted him. His breathing ragged, Seton lifted his head for a moment, his lips parted as he stared at her. Without hesitation, Lucie put her hand behind his head and drew him down to her again, returning his kiss with a fire she had never shown before.

With a cry, Seton bore her back onto the rug, raining kisses on her lips, her eyes, her throat. Then, his breath a panting gasp, he raised himself on one elbow and slowly undid the buttons of her shirt. His moan of pleasure was almost like one of pain as he looked at her breasts for the first time, seeing them young and firm, the nipples small, tight buds that tilted tantalisingly towards him. 'You're so beautiful.

So perfect.' Unable to resist, Seton bent to kiss, to touch, to arouse her into hardness and drive them both wild with frustrated longing.

'God, I want you,' he moaned. 'It's driving me crazy. I can't sleep. I can't work. I think about you all the time.'

Lucie opened eyes dark with need to look at him. 'Think about making love, do you mean?'

'Oh, yes. I *ache* for that. But I think of so much more, of—'

He broke off abruptly as Lucie reached out to his belt. 'You'll have to help me,' she said unsteadily. 'I can't manage with only one hand.'

'Lucie.' Seton stared down at her. 'Are you sure?'

She smiled at him. 'Oh, yes, I'm very sure.' And she finally admitted, 'You're not the only one who's been having sleepless nights. So why don't we make our wish come true?' she invited huskily.

There was wonder in Seton's eyes as, coming up on his knees and taking his time, delighting in every moment and saving it for ever in his memory, he took off the rest of her clothes. She looked so beautiful lying there before him. The knowledge that in a moment she would be his at last, that he would enter her and make her his own, made his breath rasp in his throat. His hands shook as he touched her, the thought of the joy and pleasure that was to come almost overwhelming. When she lay completely naked, he murmured, 'I adore you. Oh, my darling, I worship you.'

'Take me, then.' Lucie's voice grew urgent. 'Take me now!'

Slipping off his own clothes, Seton bent first to kiss her again before coming down onto her. He tried to be gentle at first, but the exquisite, agonising pleasure soon aroused him so much that he lost control. With a gasping cry, he put an arm under her hips and lifted her towards him, thrusting with such passion that Lucie cried out, her body on fire with ecstasy, her hot, panting mouth searching for his, her arms around him, holding him yet closer. The rising tide of sensuality overtook them, engulfed them, and their mingled groans of delight echoed into the air as their bodies joined in the most primitive and yet most beautiful act in the world.

When it was over they lay in each other's arms for a long time, too exhausted to move, too enraptured still by what had taken place between them to want to break the spell. Until, at length, Seton, his heart still thudding in his chest, raised an unsteady hand to move a lock of hair that clung to her damp face. When she opened her eyes and looked at him, Lucie saw the most wonderful light of happiness in his face. It shone from him, in the blaze of triumph in his eyes, in the smile of tenderness he gave her. 'That,' he said simply as he gently kissed her, 'was the most wonderful moment of my life.'

Lucie sighed softly, knowing herself completely happy and fulfilled, her body satiated with pleasure.

'And for you?' he questioned. 'Was it good for you too?' A rueful look came into his eyes. 'I didn't mean to be quite so passionate, but things kind of got out of control.'

Lifting her hand, Lucie ran her fingertips over his lips, then down to circle his minute nipples, knowing it was safe to play with him, tease him. 'I never knew before that they had earthquakes in England.'

He grinned delightedly. 'The earth moved, did it?'

'And some.' Lifting herself into a sitting position, she pushed him back onto the rug and leaned down to kiss him, her long hair shading their faces, making the kiss very intimate, very private. 'I'm glad you lost control,' she said softly, her lips against his mouth. Straightening, she let her hand move over him, caressing, exploring. 'You're so strong,' she murmured. 'Have such power.'

Taking his hands, she held her own against it, comparing their size, amazed at how much smaller hers was. Fascinated by the physical differences between them, Lucie gazed at him, at the length of his lean body, quiet now and unaroused. She ran her hand along his soft skin, from his neck down his chest and thighs, along his muscled legs to his feet. 'You're beautiful,' she said in admiration. 'I didn't know a naked man could be beautiful.'

Her hand trailed up again but found that things had changed. She gave a surprised gasp, and explored a little more until Seton couldn't bear it any longer. With a groan he pulled her under him and made love to her again.

Rowing back up the river, the evening sun casting long shadows over the water, was a moment to be held and treasured. Lucie had never felt so content, so fulfilled. And it showed in her face, in her radiant smile and the glow of happiness in her eyes. It had been a golden day in her life, a day satiated by food and wine, by sun and sex, by coming alive as a woman.

Seton found it hard to take his eyes off her, she looked so beautiful. And she looked as if she had been well and truly loved; it showed in the languid hand she trailed in the water, in the intimate smiles she gave him with languorous eyes, in the way her mouth curved and her lips parted in remembered pleasure. Just looking at her like that was an aphrodisiac, made him want her yet again.

'Do you remember,' he said, 'when I told you I wanted you? Before—well, before the wish came true, I started to say that it wasn't just making love that I wanted.'

'*Just* making love?' She smiled at him teasingly.

He grinned back at her, the triumph of winning her and of giving her such pleasure obvious in his face. 'I know. A stupid way of putting it.' His voice becoming earnest, he went on, 'But I do want more, Lucie. I want to be with you, know that you're mine. I dream of coming home to find you waiting for me. I long for the time when I won't have to drive away and leave you at the end of an evening together.' His voice grew husky. 'That tears me apart, having to leave you.'

She thought he was asking her to let him stay at the flat with her that night so that they could make love again. So she said, 'I want that too. I want you to stay whenever you can.'

They came to the boatyard and Seton concentrated on taking them neatly up against the mooring, on tying the boat up. Helping her out, he said in her ear, 'You have grass in your hair.'

'Oh.' Lucie laughed as she combed it with her fingers, and threw him a pert glance that was full of new-found confidence. He had given her femininity, and an assurance of her power to arouse him.

Collecting their picnic things, they strolled back to his car and loaded them into the boot. Seton opened the sun-roof to let the heat out and they drove to a pub and sat on the terrace overlooking the river for a drink. Over it, Seton said, 'I will stay tonight, of course, but that wasn't what I meant.' Taking her hand, he said, 'I'm head over heels in love with you, Lucie. I want to be with you for always. I want you to marry me, my darling, just as soon as we can arrange it.'

Lucie stared at him in stunned surprise, her mind whirling. 'But I—I thought you just wanted . . .'

'Oh, Lucie, how could you be so blind? Surely you must know how much I care about you?'

She pulled her hand away, a stricken look in her eyes. 'But it's too soon. We've only known each other a few weeks.'

'But what difference does that make? I know you love me; today proved that. Can you deny it? Can you, Lucie?'

Slowly she shook her head, knowing that to pretend would be useless. But she repeated, 'It's too soon.'

Lifting a hand to stroke her face, Seton said, 'I know what you're saying, but you're all wrong, my darling girl! I fell in love with you almost from the first moment. To me it was a miracle—a very wonderful miracle. And I know that there's no way in the world that I could ever stop loving you. Nothing you or anyone else can do could possibly make me change the way I feel. I'm not going to grow out of it and nor are you. Believe me, Lucie, this is for keeps.'

She stared across at him. 'You—you'll go on loving me, no matter what?' she said faintly.

Seton smiled, his eyes so full of warmth and tenderness that she knew she would hold this moment in her heart for ever. 'No matter what,' he agreed. 'Fate has thrown us together in the most remarkable manner and there's no way I'm ever going to let you go now that I've found you at last.'

Making one last, desperate effort, she said, 'We could live together, if you like. I'd give up my job and the flat and come to live with you, or else you could move in with me.'

Seton's hand tightened for a moment and there was a glow in his eyes as he said, 'I appreciate that, I really do, but what's the point? If we're going to live together, if we're so committed to each other that we want to be together all the time, then why not get married? And remember I'm nearly thirty years old. I need to get started.'

'Started on what?'

'Married life. A family.' To his delight she blushed. 'Oh, Lucie. My darling girl.' His voice softened. 'You've trusted yourself to me today, Lucie; won't you trust yourself for the rest of your life?'

For a moment a bright dream of happiness unfolded before her, so strong, almost within her grasp. 'I want to,' she said on a sigh. 'I really want to.' But her heart was troubled and she knew she had to try to be honest with him. 'But—some years ago— '

Immediately he put his fingers over her lips, silencing her. 'That was in the past. Forget it! It's only the future that matters. Our future. Are you afraid to grasp it?'

She stared at him, dimly knowing that he was wrong, that you could never entirely blot out the past, but he was so forceful, so convincing that he carried her along with him on a tide of optimism and confidence. 'No,' she said, on a high of courage. 'I'm not afraid.'

A great light of happiness came into Seton's eyes. 'Then, will you marry me, my darling, my love?'

Lucie nodded, her voice too choked up to speak. And silly tears came into her eyes before she was finally able to say, 'Yes.' Then more firmly she said, 'Yes, I will marry you.'

But in the dawn of the following morning, when Seton had left her bed and Lucie was alone, when she no longer had his strength and will-power to carry her along on a tidal wave of optimism, then all the doubts and fears came crowding back. Because she hadn't told him the truth about her past—not all of it. She hadn't told him that she had been to prison. For three long years. And now she was terribly afraid that one day he might find out, that the past might come back to haunt her.

CHAPTER ONE

As Lucie sat on the terrace watching her son as he played in the garden, the sun warm on her face, her thoughts drifted back to that summer five years ago when she and Seton had met. Now she could laugh at the fears she'd had then, knowing that marrying Seton was the best thing she'd ever done.

They had been such happy years; she knew herself to have grown in confidence, to have blossomed in the certainty of Seton's love for her. At first she had been almost afraid to trust this happiness, so many bad things having happened to her in the past that she'd felt it too good to be true, had been petrified that something would happen to take it all away from her. But as time passed, when Seton didn't suddenly change, when his parents were so warm and welcoming, treating her like a loved daughter, when she met his friends and found they accepted her as one of themselves, and—most of all—when she soon became pregnant and gave birth to Sam Lucie finally put aside her fears and became the happy, contented woman she now was.

During the first year of their marriage, she and Seton had lived in London, in his old flat which was within easy reach of his chambers, but they'd begun house-hunting as soon as she'd become pregnant, spending their weekends driving around the countryside, and had found this house almost by accident.

It was an old dower house that had been empty for some time: Georgian, built of ivy-covered stone and set in almost an acre of ground on the edge of a pretty village. Lucie had fallen in love with it at once, even though it had been neglected and would need a lot of tender, loving care lavished upon it. But she had love in abundance now and together they had transformed the house into a beautiful home set in an even lovelier garden.

Seton still had to go away quite a bit, whenever the courts were in session, but he was at home as often as possible, openly delighting in his marriage, as much in love with Lucie as ever. He was away now, not due home until that evening. Glancing at her watch, Lucie saw that it was only four o'clock, nearly three hours before he would be home, but already she was impatient to see him.

'I'm thirsty.'

Sam climbed onto her knee and made a grab for Lucie's glass of wine but was firmly given some orange juice. 'No, this is yours.'

'When can I have wine?'

'I've told you—when you're as tall as Daddy.'

He smiled at her, knowing that she was fobbing him off, not believing that he would ever be as tall as the father who towered above him. His smile was so like Seton's in the way he looked at her sometimes that Lucie's heart lurched, overpoweringly full of love for them both. Having drunk his juice, Sam slipped off her lap and went over to the nearby sun-lounger, lay on it and was almost instantly asleep.

Getting up, Lucie moved the parasol until the shadow it cast protected him from the sun's rays. Raising her hand, she pushed her hair off her cheek.

She wore it shorter now, only down to her neck, but it was still straight, just curling inwards to frame her face. Looking down at her son, she felt a great wave of love and protectiveness. She was so glad she'd married Seton. So glad. Her eyes filled with tears of gratitude, and she lifted a finger to wipe them dry.

'Hey, what's this?'

Lucie turned at the sound of his familiar voice and found her husband framed by the open French windows. 'Seton!' With a joyful cry she ran to him and he caught her in his arms, lifting her off her feet and spinning her round, then bending his head to kiss her, still holding her off the ground.

'Daddy! Daddy!'

Looking down, Seton saw that Sam had woken and he, too, had come running to greet him, clamouring for attention by pulling at his trouser leg. Laughing, he put Lucie down but kept his arm round her waist as he stooped to lift Sam so that his little face was level with his own. He was rewarded with a kiss on his cheek and the clasp of two chubby arms that went round his neck.

'You're home so early! I didn't expect you for hours.'

'They agreed to settle out of court, thank goodness. So I was able to get away and surprise you. And I find you in tears! What on earth's the matter?'

She wrinkled her nose. 'Oh, I was just getting maudlin.'

'I'd better kiss you into feeling better, then.'

'You've already had enough kisses.'

'Nonsense. A man can't have too many kisses. You remember that, Sam.'

'OK,' his son said happily, and gave him another, very noisy kiss, which made them laugh.

'Sit down and I'll get you a drink,' Lucie invited. 'Then you can tell me about the case.'

Seton sat down in her vacated chair, Sam on his lap, and accepted the drink gratefully. But he didn't talk about the case, beyond repeating that it had been settled to his client's advantage. He never did talk about his cases in detail; to Seton, being a lawyer was like being a doctor: anything told to him was always in complete confidence.

He dealt in civil law not criminal, and sometimes cases—fraud, for example—could last quite a while, so it was always good when they finished earlier than expected. Sam was looking at him expectantly, although he didn't ask, and after a few minutes Seton smiled, reached into his pocket and brought out a wrapped parcel which he gave to the boy. Sam opened it excitedly, to reveal a brightly coloured pencil with a rubber figure fixed on the top. He gave a crow of pleasure, gave his father another kiss, then demanded that Lucie find him some paper he could draw on.

When he was settled at the table, Seton opened his briefcase and took out a bottle of scent for Lucie.

She had pulled another chair up close to his and took his hand as she leaned forward to thank him. Their eyes met, held, were full of promise. 'How did you know I'd almost run out?'

He smiled at her lazily. 'It's noticing things like that that earns a man Brownie points.' Getting to his feet, Seton drew Lucie back inside the house, his eyes already darkening as he took her into his arms to kiss her hungrily. 'God, I've missed you,' he muttered against her mouth.

'It's only been a few days,' Lucie laughed.

'Nearer a week. A whole week of loneliness, of wanting you, longing for you. Of dreaming about you.' He was kissing her as he spoke, on her throat, the line of her jaw, pushing aside the top of her dress to kiss and caress the fullness of her breasts. 'Let's go to bed,' he said thickly.

Returning his embrace with a passion fuelled by her own longing, Lucie said, 'It's so early. What about Sam?'

'He's happy enough for the moment. Come on. *Come on!*'

She let him take her by the hand and lead her upstairs to their bedroom. There was no need to draw the curtains; the house was too isolated for anyone to see. Immediately they were inside they began to undress each other, as eager for this as they had always been, time and familiarity having in no way diminished the fire that swept through them as they touched, clung, caressed.

'My darling. My love.' Seton was on his knees before her, taking off the last of her clothes. He kissed her deeply, so intimately that Lucie threw back her head in a long, uncontrollable moan. He rose, his hands sliding up her legs and thighs, his breath already rasping in anticipation. For a moment he held her close against him, letting her feel the hardness of his arrant masculinity, of his desperate need for her.

It drove them both wild.

'Seton!' Lucie moved against him. 'I want you so much. Please. Please.'

With a groan he carried her to the bed, laid her on it and, too eager for finesse, immediately took her, entering her welcoming warmth with abandoned pleasure. Lucie arched to meet him, feeling his hot skin against her own, their panting, moaning breaths mingling as they kissed, her arms around him as she held him close.

It was always like this when he had been away, their eagerness to make love, this almost savage urgency. Lucie felt excitement flare, cried out his name as the exquisite pleasure increased, until it engulfed her entirely and the whole wonderful world was contained in this long moment of ecstatic sensuality.

They made love again later that night, after putting Sam to bed and eating a leisurely dinner together. In some ways that second time was almost as exciting as the first, because they knew it was going to happen, because they deliberately prolonged the moment until they went up to their bedroom again. Lucie bathed, put on a long white nightdress that was almost demure and sat at her dressing table to brush her hair. But Seton took the brush from her, as he loved to do, and made each stroke one of admiration and intimacy.

This time they made love far more slowly, each knowing what the other liked most, what gave them the greatest excitement and pleasure. Lucie lay alongside Seton, kissing and caressing his length, making him sigh deeply and gasp in sensual delight as he found it too wonderful to stop her but almost unbearable to wait. She smiled, knowing just how far to go to tantalise him, then bent to kiss his mouth.

It was Seton's turn then, to tease a little, to toy with her until her fingers bit into his shoulders and she gave little, animal moans of mingled pleasure and frustration. He could wait no longer. With a swift movement he leaned back on the bed and pulled her astride him. 'Now, my darling. Now!' And, holding her waist, he gave her the overwhelming pleasure he knew she loved.

Moonlight played across the crumpled bed. Lucie found her nightdress but tossed it aside, wanting to feel her own nakedness against Seton's for the rest of the night. He lay on his side behind her and put his arms round her in the protective way in which they always slept. 'My darling.' He kissed her shoulder. 'My beautiful, wonderful wife. You can't possibly know how much I adore you.'

Lucie smiled in the darkness and settled more comfortably into his hold. 'Do you think we made a baby?'

'I certainly hope so.' His arm tightened round her. 'I long for a little girl, just like you.' He chuckled. 'We certainly gave it our best shot.' Pushing her hair aside, he kissed her neck, but then yawned tiredly. 'Goodnight, my love.'

Within a few minutes he was asleep, but Lucie lay awake in the darkness, wondering if the miracle had happened and they would have another child. It was time that Sam had a brother, or the sister that Seton so wanted for him, and as all she wanted was Seton's happiness then that was what Lucie wanted too. She loved him so much, so very much.

Sometimes, when she reluctantly looked into her past, it seemed that her life had only really begun on the blessed day when she had met him. All the years before then counted as nothing, were like some terrible nightmare from which she had woken to find herself in a living paradise. In all those years of her youth and childhood there had been only one good thing and that had been Kate Brownlow, the woman Lucie called Aunt Kate and whose surname she had taken, but who wasn't her real aunt at all, although Seton thought she was.

Kate had been a prison visitor; she was a mature and kind woman who had recognised Lucie's basic honesty and believed in her innocence. She had taken Lucie under her wing, encouraged her to take educational courses, and given her a home until she could find work and afford her flat in Hayford. For that Lucie was eternally grateful, and she looked on Aunt Kate as a dear relation, the only person who knew the whole truth about her, and who had sworn, albeit reluctantly, never to tell Seton.

Lucie sighed, pushing thoughts of the past from her mind. They seldom came back to haunt her now; the present was too full, too happy. She rolled onto her back and Seton's arm went across her. He murmured something in his sleep, said it again and she understood. 'Love you, Lucie.'

She smiled and looked at his face, lit by the moonlight. He had given many of his features to his son. His mother had shown Lucie photographs of Seton taken when he had been the same age and it was incredible how alike they looked. She was glad that Sam would look and be like him; she had been too wary of her own genes to feel confident in passing them on.

His hair had fallen forward over his forehead; gently Lucie pushed it back. Her touch had been feather-light but even so his lashes fluttered and Seton said, 'Why aren't you asleep?' She didn't answer and he opened his eyes. 'You ought to be worn out.' Still she didn't speak and he sighed. 'You are an insatiable woman. At this rate I shall be a burnt-out shell by the time I'm forty.' But he smiled as he drew her to him and began to make love to her again.

This time she slept for a while afterwards, but woke to find the room in complete darkness, the moonlight gone. Seton was deeply asleep, his breath even and regular. Lucie tried to work out how many times they'd made love since they'd known each other, but couldn't begin to count. It was possible to work out how many days they'd known each other so intimately, but they had made love more than once in a day so often—frequently even three times or more, as tonight—that it was impossible to say.

But repetition had never staled their lovemaking. It had always been so good, so breathtaking. And the joy had always been shared; there had never been the slightest need of pretence at fulfilment, as some women she'd read about resorted to, and as some of her women friends had confided. With Seton the excitement had always been true and wonderful, both of them delighting the other, and their own pleasure the greater because of it.

Their marriage was perfect in every way. Too perfect, perhaps. Lucie knew that Seton put her on a pedestal, that his love for her fell little short of adoration. It frightened her sometimes, the force and depth of his feelings. But that was only when she allowed herself to think about it; most of the time she was just full of heartfelt thanks for having met him, for his having fallen so hopelessly in love with her.

In return she tried to make their marriage, their lives as happy and content as she possibly could. Whatever Seton had wanted she would have done; she would have devoted her life to him completely, but he'd insisted on her finishing her Open University course, and when she got an honours degree he'd encouraged her to find a job as a part-time teacher. Lucie had given that up when Sam was born, but hoped one day to go back to teaching art.

Her life was perfect, the past buried deep—and Lucie knew that she would do anything to keep it that way.

They went for a holiday to Norway, the first they'd taken abroad as a family, and it was a great success, Sam loving every minute. Lucie returned with a gorgeous tan, and the hope that she was pregnant again, which was a tremendous joy to them both.

For a while it was to be their secret, until they were absolutely sure, but the knowledge increased Lucie's vivacity as the tan increased her beauty. At twenty-seven she was in the prime of womanhood, her body slender but rounded, her pale gold hair a fitting frame for her lovely face and eyes so full of life and happiness. It was hardly any wonder that Seton looked at her with such pride of possession, even less wonder that he couldn't keep his hands off, that he made love to her at every opportunity.

Shortly after they got back Lucie and half a dozen of her friends—those like herself with young children and who regularly got together for morning coffee—decided to have a day out by themselves. A day off from husbands, children and responsibilities. They would go to Ladies' Day at Ascot, have a champagne picnic, wear new outfits, outrageous hats, the lot.

'I'm jealous,' Seton complained as he watched her try on her outfit the day before their outing. 'You'll be having a wonderful time while I'm stuck in a stuffy old court listening to a man who is clearly guilty try to lie his way out of paying a hefty settlement.' He was sitting on their bed, propped up against the headboard, still fascinated to watch her dress.

'Tough,' Lucie answered. 'They only have one Ladies' Day; you can go any time.'

'But I really think I ought to be there to look after you. You look so lovely that you'll have admiring men flocking around you like bees at a honeypot. And you happen to be *my* honeypot.'

'For your private consumption, huh?'

'Definitely.'

Lucie put on the jacket of her burnt orange and white suit, then added the hat, wide-brimmed but turned up at the front and adorned with big orange and white silk flowers.

He groaned. 'Take it all off. I'm not going to let you go. You look just too lovely. Some stinking rich millionaire will probably fall at your feet, then carry you off to his yacht or his stately home.'

Lucie smiled, pretending to like the idea. 'Sounds pretty good to me.'

Seton growled at her. 'If any man touches you I'll tear him apart.'

She turned to face him. 'Such caveman stuff. Do I really look all right?'

'My darling girl.' Getting up, he came over to her and turned her to face the mirror. 'Can't you believe the evidence of your own eyes? You will outshine every woman there.'

Meeting his gaze in their reflection, Lucie said, 'I'm not going for that. We're just going for a giggle. But I wish you were coming. I want to share everything with you.'

Recognising an unsure note in her voice, Seton put his hands on her shoulders and gently turned her towards him. 'You will have the most wonderful time with your friends,' he said firmly. 'You will bet on all the races and win a fortune. You will have a most delicious picnic and drink lots of champagne. And when you come home I will whisk you upstairs, take off all your clothes except that fantastic hat and then make love to you exactly where you're standing now, in front of the mirror.' She flushed, as he'd known she would, in the way that still delighted him.

She moved away, began to change back into her ordinary clothes. 'Your mother has been dropping hints about us having another baby; she'll be so pleased when we tell her.'

'Of course; my parents have found a new lease of life since they've become grandparents.'

She laughed. 'They might not be quite so keen after they've had Sam all day tomorrow.'

'And overnight,' Seton grinned.

Lucie gave him an old-fashioned look. 'When did you arrange that?'

'I haven't yet—but I'm certainly going to now that I've seen you in that hat.'

'You're incorrigible.'

'It's your own fault, woman; you shouldn't be so sensational.' And he kissed her again.

The next day was warm and sunny but without a breeze, exactly right for all those hats. As Seton had predicted, Lucie had a wonderful time. They had a stretch limo to take them to the racecourse and set out their picnic in the car park, alongside all the Rolls-Royces and Bentleys. Because they were all women together they could let their hair down and there was a lot of laughter, especially after they'd opened the second bottle of champagne. Lucie was enjoying herself as much as the others until a photographer she hadn't noticed came along and took a shot of them all as they clustered round the frothing bottle of bubbly with their glasses.

'That was a good one,' the photographer remarked. 'It might be accepted by a paper. Give me your names for the caption, ladies.'

Lucie hesitated but decided to be cautious. 'I don't want my name in a newspaper,' she said to Anna, the friend next to her. 'Please see that he doesn't get it.' And she got to her feet and walked quickly away.

When she got back ten minutes later the man had gone.

'You didn't give him my name, did you?' she asked, trying to sound casual.

'No.' Anna hesitated. 'But Fiona talked to him, gave him her name. I think she's a bit squiffy,' she admitted. 'But don't worry; why on earth would they put us in the paper when they've got all these beautiful women and outfits to choose from?'

Which was very true. They packed away the picnic, walked down to watch the races, and Lucie forgot about the photographer in the excitement of picking two winners.

And Seton kept his promise—more than fulfilled it as he made love to her that night in front of the mirror, their passion for each other seeming to be doubled as they not only felt but saw themselves giving and taking such glorious pleasure. 'Hold your hat on, sweetheart,' Seton groaned out. 'Because I'm going to blow your mind.'

That made Lucie start to laugh, but soon she was gasping, her eyes closing in exquisite sensuality then opening to see their straining bodies in the mirror. She moaned, the eroticism of it almost too much to bear, and then cried out in ecstasy as Seton lifted her off the ground and held her to him. They were free tonight, with Sam not there, to give voice to their excitement, to cry out the other's name, to give full rein to a hunger that was heightened but never satiated.

Lucie woke late the next morning, able to sleep in because Sam wasn't there and Seton didn't have to go to work. She showered and dressed, taking her time, smiling when she saw her discarded hat on the floor. Carefully she packed it away in her wardrobe, sentimentally thinking that she would keep it for ever, take it out when they were old and grey and smile in happy remembrance of the past night.

Seton had made breakfast and was sitting in their big, sunlit kitchen reading the paper. He glanced at the back page then gave an exclamation of astonishment. 'Lucie! Your picture's in the paper!'

'What?'

She looked over his shoulder as he held the paper for her to see. It made a good photograph, in colour, all of them in their chic outfits, laughing and happy as they held out their glasses to catch the fountain of bubbles like diamonds in the sun. Lucie was in the forefront, easily recognisable, the most attractive of them all, and her name was clearly given, along with the name of the village from which they all came.

Seton said, 'How amazing. You didn't tell me you'd had it taken.'

'I forgot. There were so many beautiful women there, and lots of photographers going around. I didn't think they'd ever print it.'

'But it's a wonderful shot. You all look so happy.' He grinned at her and put his arm round her waist. 'I told you you'd be the most beautiful woman there.'

She gave him a hug and sat opposite him, helping herself to cereals, looking across at the photograph as Seton read the rest of the paper. Her heart sank a little and Lucie wondered if she had changed much over the last ten years. Would anyone who had known her then recognise the same person in the sophisticated young woman in the picture? On the whole she thought not, and they certainly wouldn't recognise the name of Lucie Wallace, of course. That thought made Lucie feel considerably better, enough to make her laugh at her fears as absurd. She was safe now—safe and secure in the world that Seton had given her.

He gave a sound of disdain and read out an item from the paper that had caught his eye. He often did this, keeping up with the news, especially with politics, and frequently made some quite scathing remarks when he disagreed with something. Often, though, he read out items that amused him too, or that aroused his sympathy. 'You must read this piece,' he told her, a few minutes later. 'It's a report on how women drivers can take steps to protect themselves if they break down when they're alone.'

'You've already given me a mobile phone.'

'Wouldn't hurt to read it, though.'

Lucie smiled, knowing that his most anxious concern was always for her safety and well-being.

He made another angry sound. 'They'll have to do something about the overcrowding in the prisons.

There's a piece here about a man who shot a policeman actually being allowed out four years early. He was sentenced to fifteen years but has only served eleven.'

The jug of fruit juice that Lucie was holding slipped dangerously in her hand as her blood ran cold. 'R-really? What—what was his name?' Somehow she managed to say the words although her voice seemed somehow disembodied, not part of herself any more.

'What?' Seton's eyes had already moved on, but he looked back at the item. Even before he spoke she somehow knew what he was going to say. The premonition was so strong that she felt no surprise when he said, 'Some foreign name. Oh, yes, here it is. Rick Ravena.'

He went on to say something else but Lucie didn't hear him; time seemed to have stopped. It was the only name in all the world that she had hoped never to hear again, the name of the man who had ruined her life, whose vindictiveness had sent her to prison for something she hadn't done.

CHAPTER TWO

Lucie went on automatically pouring the orange juice, but her hand was shaking now and she slopped some onto the table. Quickly she got up to get a cloth, turned her back on Seton so that he couldn't see her face.

He glanced at his watch. 'We'd better get a move on; remember, we're booked for a game of tennis at the club before we pick up Sam from my parents.'

Lucie desperately wanted to be alone, to try and come to terms with this terrible news. She thought about saying that she didn't feel up to playing tennis, but knew that Seton would insist on staying with her if she felt unwell. So perhaps it would be better to go; at least they would be among other people, so that Seton's attention would be distracted from her. They were so close that she was very afraid that he would notice there was something wrong.

Most of the girls who'd been to Ascot the previous day were at the club, revelling in their brief hour of fame. Anna saw them arrive and immediately came over. 'Have you seen the paper? Isn't it wonderful?' She kissed Lucie on the cheek but Seton on the mouth, her eyes smiling up at him. 'I'm going to phone the newspaper and ask them to let me have a copy of the photo to frame.'

'A great idea,' Seton enthused. 'Perhaps you could get one for us as well?'

'Of course.' Anna slipped her arm through Seton's and led him over to a fixtures list on the wall. 'Look, we've been drawn together in the Draw for a Partner tournament.'

Seton looked at the list but soon came back to Lucie. She raised a strained face to his and he frowned. 'Is anything the matter, darling?'

She managed to give a hollow little laugh. 'Anna's flirting with you again.'

He shrugged. 'Anna flirts with everybody.'

But Lucie shook her head. 'She fancies you.'

'Good heavens, you're not worried about it, are you?' Seton said in amazement. 'You must know that it doesn't mean a thing to me. No other woman in the world even exists when I have you.'

He said it simply, his feelings utterly genuine and plain to read. It made Lucie feel humble but so wonderfully secure in his love for her. But she was secure in nothing else, her peace of mind shattered by news of Rick Ravena's freedom. It was because of it, because she was feeling so pulverised that she'd even mentioned Anna's manner. She'd always known that the other girl liked Seton, even though she had a husband of her own, and usually she just ignored it, but today she was feeling too tense to just let it go.

They played their match and lost, Lucie playing badly, unable to concentrate on the game. Afterwards Seton put a comforting arm round her shoulders and whispered in her ear, 'I'm not surprised you haven't any energy after last night.'

For a brief moment she didn't understand, then managed to give him a rather unsteady smile as she bitterly realised that this news of Rick had driven the memory of their wonderful night together completely from her mind.

The clubhouse had a small restaurant attached to it; after they'd showered they went into it and Anna, who was sitting at a table by the big picture windows with her husband, Martin, immediately waved to them, indicating that she'd saved seats for them.

Anna and Martin were, Lucie supposed, their closest friends in the village. They lived only half a mile away and their circumstances were similar, each couple having just the one child, both boys and the same age. The two women often babysat for each other or looked after the two boys during the day if one of them needed to go out alone. They were close friends, yet Lucie sometimes sensed that Anna was jealous of her, of her marriage to Seton which was so obviously happy. In some ways it was a one-sided friendship because Anna was the confiding type, often complaining about Martin who, she said, wasn't very virile. Lucie, on the other hand, never discussed her marriage, but then she had absolutely nothing to complain about—entirely the opposite in fact.

Usually they all chatted amicably together, but today, although Lucie tried her best, her thoughts were continuously elsewhere and she often fell silent. Their meal over, with Lucie's plate hardly touched, Seton gave her a frowning glance and said firmly, 'I'm afraid we have to go and pick up Sam.'

'Oh, you don't have to go yet, surely?' Anna put a hand on Seton's arm. 'We could have another match.'

'Lucie's feeling tired.'

Anna gave Lucie a speculative look. 'Yes, you do look awfully pale. Are you all right?'

'Fine,' Lucie lied. 'As Seton said, I'm just a little tired.'

They went to collect Sam but Seton's mother insisted they stay to tea, and to refuse would have been unfair after all their kindness, so it was early evening before they got home, by which time Lucie was so tense with trying to pretend that there was nothing the matter that she felt close to screaming point.

Looking at her set face, Seton frowned. 'I have that meeting to go to tonight, but you don't look at all well; would you like me to put it off?'

Lucie gave an almost audible sigh of relief. 'No, of course not. I'm going to have a bath and go to bed early. I'll be fine.'

She knew that the meeting tonight was important so she was able to persuade him to go, and as he left she thought that, God help her, for the first time in her life she was glad that he wasn't going to be there, that she could be alone.

After she had gone through the now familiar ceremony of putting Sam to bed—of giving him his bath, talking through the day, and then reading him two stories—Lucie was at last free to seek the comfort of her own bed, to lie there in the darkness, her fevered mind a prey to fears and memories.

She hadn't thought about the past for a long time—from the moment of her marriage she had deliberately put it out of her mind—but this morning it had all come flooding rudely back. Lucie bitterly resented the intrusion of the past into the present. She had long ago stopped thinking about Rick Ravena, had even stopped comparing Seton's family life and upbringing with her own.

An only child, he had been so fortunate to have close, loving parents. They had given him a wonderful home, a good education and made sure that he had a full knowledge of the world and what it had to offer. Any talents he had shown had been encouraged, so that he was good at sports and much else besides. But they had been careful not to smother him, and had given him the degree of independence that had made him into the confident, supremely assured man that he was today.

Her own upbringing had been a stark contrast. Her mother had deserted her and her father when she was very young. 'Gone off with some damn stud and saddled me with her brat,' her father had often railed. If he had been her real father. Sometimes, when he'd had too much to drink, he had gone on about her not being like him. 'You're too bloody clever to be mine,' he'd mutter. 'Too bloody clever by half.' And he'd often accused her of driving her mother away, which had deeply upset Lucie as a child, when she hadn't understood what had happened. She had been made to feel guilty but hadn't known why, so had drawn into herself in defence.

But her father must have cared for her in his way because he'd kept her with him, even marrying again to have a woman to look after her. But that hadn't lasted long and he'd got divorced. After that there had been several other women he'd lived with but not married, who had treated Lucie with varying degrees of rough kindness or outright resentment, until he'd finally got married for the third time to a woman who already had three young children of her own.

Lucie had been very bright at school, finding more peace and interest outside her home than she'd ever

found in it, and she'd worked hard because the only
praise she'd ever got was from her teachers. There
had been talk of her being university material, but
that had soon stopped after her father had firmly said
that she was leaving the minute she was old enough
to go out to work. But he had died when she was
fourteen, falling off a ladder and landing on his head.
For a few months he had been in Intensive Care, but
his brain had been virtually dead, and in the end
they'd turned off the life-support machines and he'd
died of pneumonia soon afterwards.

Even now Lucie couldn't think about the hell the
next year had been, as she was made to look after her
stepbrothers and sister while her stepmother went out
every night, having to do all the housework and often
being kept off school. She was hit, and hit hard, for
the slightest misdemeanour, or even for no reason
other than that her stepmother was in a bad mood
and felt like it. But she was given a roof over her head
until the longed-for sixteenth birthday arrived, and
she left the same day, travelling down to London to
stay at the YWCA and get herself a job.

Her big ambition had been to go to evening classes,
to take courses so that she could better herself and
never be dependent on anyone again. But it didn't
work out like that. Lucie had only been in London a
couple of weeks when she met Rick. He chatted her
up in a coffee-bar, and straight away her life was
transformed into something exciting and glamorous.
He had a fast car, a flat of his own, and always enough
money to take her out to clubs and discos. Her ambitions were forgotten as Lucie fell under his domi-
nating spell, and soon she would have done anything
he wanted.

The first thing Rick wanted was, of course, to go to bed with her. Because she'd been so withdrawn at school, so busy working in her home all the rest of the time, Lucie had never even had a boyfriend before. She thought that Rick was in love with her, believed him when he said so, and didn't resist very much when he gave her too much to drink one night and took her virginity.

He made her as much a slave as she had been to her stepmother, but she was still innocent of mind and didn't realise that the little errands he sent her on were illegal, that on the nights when they sat necking in his car parked in a quiet residential street he was actually watching the houses, working out which would be good prospects to break into. He was kind to her in an offhand way, and made sure he kept her dependent on him so that she was unable to leave him.

Then came the terrible night when a neighbour saw him entering a house and called the police. By then Lucie had been living with him for almost three months, and on that particular night he took her with him. He left her in the car, saying that he had to meet someone on business. It might even have been true, but Rick saw an open window in a darkened house and wasn't able to resist breaking in.

Lucie was tired and had dozed, not waking until she heard the commotion and saw Rick come rushing towards her. But a policeman raced after him. Lucie didn't know that Rick had a gun. He shot the poor policeman twice then threw his loot away and escaped through an alleyway, abandoning Lucie to her fate. Perhaps he'd thought that she was so besotted by him that she wouldn't tell the police who he was, and maybe she wouldn't have done if they hadn't taken her to see the policeman in hospital for herself, all wired up to machines and drips, fighting for his life.

She told them everything then, answered all their questions, completely devastated, her eyes opened to the life she'd been leading, to the even more terrible life she was heading for. She had to stand trial, but the police assured her that she'd get off lightly because this was her first offence and because she'd helped them. They were been kind enough, but she was kept in custody and didn't see Rick again until the trial.

He knew there was no hope for him after she gave her testimony, but she never forgot the venom in his eyes as he looked at her. So then he did his best to implicate her, saying that she'd always known about the gun, that she'd helped him on lots of burglaries. Lucie protested her innocence but the jury believed him, and maybe the judge was having a bad day, because he sent her to prison too, for three years. Rick laughed at that, kept on laughing as they took him away to the cells.

The solicitor she'd been given wanted Lucie to appeal against the sentence, but she was so completely intimidated by what had happened to her, was so overcome by misery that she did nothing. She withdrew yet deeper into herself, lived in a kind of stupor, doing what she was told, just going around like a zombie. But then Kate Brownlow was appointed as her prison visitor and gradually everything changed for the better and led to her meeting Seton.

But Aunt Kate had been right, Lucie thought; the older woman had tried hard to persuade her to tell Seton of her past, but Lucie had been so afraid that it would spoil things, had been so intimidated by his background and his job, that she hadn't listened, instead had begged Kate to keep her secret, made her promise never to tell.

Should she confess everything to Seton now? Lucie wondered fretfully. She didn't want to. He had always thought that there was complete openness between them. What would he think when he knew that she had deceived him like this? But he loved her, and surely he would understand?

She tossed anxiously in the bed, wondering what to do, afraid of losing the perfect happiness they shared. One moment she decided that she would tell him, the next that she couldn't possibly. Her mind filled with apprehension when she thought how appalled Seton would be that he, a barrister, had a wife who had been to prison, that his son had an ex-convict for a mother. No matter that she had been innocent of any crime, that stain was on her record and always would be.

Lucie realised she'd been living in a fool's paradise—but had anything really changed? she thought, more hopefully. OK, Rick was out of prison, but why should that make any difference to her? They might still go on as they had always done, and then she would have told Seton for no reason at all. She didn't know what to do and thumped the pillows in angry indecision. But she remembered her aunt telling her it was always best to be completely honest, and she had almost made up her mind that she must tell him when he finally came home at last.

She was still lying awake in the darkness, dreading having to tell him, and trying from somewhere to find the courage.

'Are you asleep?' he murmured. Lucie didn't answer but he knew she wasn't. He undressed, slipped into bed and reached for her.

She opened her mouth to speak, to tell him everything, but then sensed a feeling of excitement in him. 'What is it?'

'My meeting tonight—it was at the local political party headquarters. The sitting MP wants to retire before the next election so they have to choose a candidate to replace him. They decided they want a local man. They asked me if I would be interested.'

Lucie sat up with a jerk and switched on the light. She had been right; there was a blaze of excitement in Seton's eyes. 'What did you say?' she asked hollowly.

'That I would have to think about it, discuss it with you.'

'But you want to do it.' It wasn't a question.

There was no hesitation in his voice as Seton said, 'Yes. It would be a beginning, Lucie. And who knows what it might lead to? Think of the challenge. Think how exciting life could be.'

She groped at straws. 'You might not get elected.'

'I might not even get picked as the candidate.' He took her hand. 'I'd like to take a shot at it. But it's entirely up to you. If you hate the idea I'll forget it, of course. You must want it as much as I do; it must be a joint thing. Aspiring candidates are judged on their wives as much as on their own merits.'

'But what if I'm pregnant? What if you want another baby?' was all Lucie could think of to say.

Seton laughed. 'Even MPs are capable of fathering children. If you'd like a demonstration...'

He reached to pull her down to kiss her, but for the first time since their marriage she pushed him away. 'You really want this, don't you?'

'Yes. Very much. What do you say?'

She switched off the light, not wanting him to see the worry in her eyes. 'I'll think about it.'

But that wasn't what she thought about as she heard him fall asleep beside her. Seton had seldom asked anything of her; it had always been he who had given her everything she wanted. But now he was asking for this great commitment from her, asking her to back him in something that he really wanted. And such a career would be exactly right for him; he would make a hard-working, dedicated MP. But who would want him if they knew that she had been to prison? If she told Seton tonight, he would immediately back down, withdraw his name. He would lose his one chance to achieve the ambition of a lifetime—and all because she had let him down.

Lucie put off giving him a decision for as long as she could. Seton was very patient but the local party wasn't and demanded an answer. There was only one she could give; Lucie had known that all along. Maybe she had been waiting for a miracle, for the party or Seton to change his mind, but life was short on miracles. She agreed that he should go ahead, that he should try to fulfil his ambition.

Only a short time later, when Seton had been selected to contest the next election, the phone rang while Lucie was doing the housework one afternoon. 'Hello?'

'Mrs Lucie Wallace?' It was a man's voice, stiff, formal.

'Yes. Who's calling?'

The voice changed, became silky, the London accent showing as the man said, 'Why, Lucie, darlin', don't you remember me?'

And she knew that Rick Ravena had found her.

CHAPTER THREE

LUCIE stood completely frozen, numb with shock. But then Rick started to speak again and she immediately slammed down the phone. All the strength seemed to have gone from her legs and Lucie staggered out of the kitchen, her arms held out before her, like a blind person groping her way.

Reaching the downstairs cloakroom, she leaned against the wall, fighting sickness, her breath coming in agonised gasps of terror and despair. Dimly she heard the phone start to ring again and then stop as the answering machine cut in. Panic seized her. She mustn't let him leave a message. She had to stop him.

Half running, half falling, Lucie went into Seton's study, crashed down onto her knees and yanked the plug of the answering machine from its socket. Then, with hands that were shaking uncontrollably, she scrabbled at the machine, sobbing in frustration when she couldn't open it at first, but at last took out the cassette. Still on her knees, she crawled back into the kitchen, pulled things haphazardly out of a cupboard until she found a large saucepan. Her breath still coming in moaning sobs, Lucie tore the endless snake of tape loose from the cassette, put it in the saucepan and somehow managed to find the matches and set light to it.

Leaning back against a cupboard, she watched the tape flame, tears running down her face and choked by sobs. She put her head in her hands, knowing that her peace was broken, her happiness gone. For about half an hour Lucie just sat there, crouched into herself, but then she heard the clock in the hall strike four and knew that Sam, who was at Anna's house playing with her son, Adam, would be brought home soon.

She mustn't let him see her like this, mustn't let Anna realise that anything was wrong. Hauling herself to her feet, Lucie picked up the saucepan and took the remains of the cassette out to the dustbin, burying it deep. The saucepan went into the dishwasher and she found a new cassette for the answering machine, managing somehow to record a message.

An idea occurred to her and she rang the phone company, told them she wanted her number changed immediately. They were unhelpful at first, but when Lucie threatened to go to another company they agreed to change the number the following day and to make it ex-directory. She left the receiver off and went upstairs to wash her face.

Lifting her head, she saw herself in the mirror on the bathroom cabinet. All the colour had drained from her face; she looked ill, punch-drunk. Oh, God, she thought, with a dejection close to anger. Why? Why have you done this to me? Hadn't she been punished enough? She'd served her sentence; why couldn't she be left in peace? Because you lied, some inner voice accused her. Because you lied to Seton.

With a moan she thrust the thought away. Her hands still unsteady, Lucie put on some make-up, trying to hide her pallor under a bright, painted mask. Luckily Seton was away on circuit and wasn't due back until the weekend. Lucie's mind stopped short and she gave a gasp of horror; never before had she been glad that Seton was away. The call from Rick Ravena had come only a hour ago and already her thinking, her priorities had changed for the worse. But what else could you expect when evil was let loose in your life?

Going into the sitting-room, Lucie knelt on the window-seat, watching out for the car that would bring Sam home. She desperately needed him now, needed the comfort of his solid little body held close in her arms, the sound of his innocent prattle in her ears to drown out the sound of that other voice. The drive, partially screened by fir trees, curved away towards the gate and the road. A figure, only dimly seen, walked along the road, looking towards the house, then seemed to pause at the open gate.

Lucie's hair seemed to stand on end as she suddenly realised that if Rick had her telephone number then he would also know her address. The figure turned into the drive, began to walk towards the house. It was a man, quite tall, his features hidden by the upturned collar of his coat. Lucie drew back, her heart pounding so much that she felt faint.

The man reached the door, rang the bell. With a sudden surge of rage, Lucie ran into the hall and flung the door open. It wasn't Rick. The man was much older, dressed in clean but shabby clothes.

'Sorry to disturb you, but I was wondering if you needed any odd jobs or gardening done? I can turn my hand to anything and—'

Lucie, usually so kind and understanding to the underprivileged, who had been there herself and knew what it was like, shouted, 'No! Go away,' and slammed the door in the man's face.

Hurriedly, she bolted the door, put the safety-catch on, then leaned against it trembling all over. Lucie tried to steady herself, took deep breaths, told herself that she was overreacting. Above her head, the bell rang again, startling her out of her skin, making her give a scream of fright. 'Go away!' she yelled through the door. 'I told you to go away!'

'Lucie?' Anna's voice sounded from the other side. 'Lucie, are you all right?'

With a sob of relief Lucie undid the bolt and chain and opened the door to find Anna gazing at her in concern.

'What on earth's the matter?'

'Oh. I . . . Nothing.'

'It doesn't look like nothing. You look terrible.'

'Mummy?' Sam, standing beside her, stepped forward and took hold of Lucie's hand. His little face was troubled as he looked up at her.

Bending, Lucie swept him up into her arms—not such an easy task now that he was four years old. 'It's OK,' she reassured him, trying to smile, to keep her voice light. 'I was just being silly, that's all.'

They went inside, Lucie still carrying Sam because she needed to have him close, but she made herself put him down when they reached the kitchen.

Anna wrinkled her nose. 'I can smell burning.'

'Yes, I—I burnt some toast,' Lucie lied in desperation.

'Toast at this time of the day?'

'Late lunch.' She turned away. 'Go and hang your coat up in the cupboard, Sam, and then find your slippers.'

Sam went off happily; he was such a good child, so content, always so obedient.

'So what was that scene at the door all about?' Anna demanded as soon as he was out of earshot.

'A man came to the door. I didn't like the look of him,' Lucie fabricated.

'Have you phoned the police?'

'No, of course not.' Lucie tried to laugh it off, having visions of the poor man being hounded. 'I'm sure he was perfectly harmless. He just took me by surprise, really. I thought it was you, you see, and... Like I told Sam, I was just being silly.'

'But still, if he's going round all the houses frightening people—'

'He wasn't! It was just me,' Lucie cut in sharply. Then she bit her lips. 'Sorry, I'm a bit on edge today.'

'Oh, I know just how you feel,' Anna agreed in heartfelt tones. 'Why, only last month...' She started on a rather involved anecdote and Lucie waited as patiently as she could for her to finish, not listening, wanting only to be alone. But Anna was in a chatty mood and it was nearly an hour before she left. Usually, when Seton was away, Lucie was glad of her friend's company, but today she gave Anna no encouragement to stay and shut the door behind her with profound relief.

But having to act normally, as if nothing had happened to turn her world upside down, had helped. It had made the panic subside a little so that Lucie was able to think. She gave Sam his supper then let him watch one of his videos while she went back into the kitchen and called Aunt Kate.

'He must have seen that photo of me in the paper,' she said miserably, after she'd explained what had happened.

'You must get your number changed at once,' her aunt advised.

'I've already put that in hand. But it's going to be so difficult now that Seton has been selected as the next parliamentary candidate; all sorts of people keep phoning him up.'

'Well, that can't be helped. You'll have to tell Seton that you've been having nuisance calls.'

Which was true enough, Lucie thought grimly. 'What shall I do? Can't he be stopped?'

'Did he threaten you or anything?'

'No, I put the phone down on him,' Lucie admitted. 'And when he rang again and left a message on the ansaphone I destroyed the tape before I listened to it.'

'Oh, dear, that wasn't such a good idea. If he didn't actually threaten you, then there's not much that we can do. Except to have your number changed, and you've already done that.'

'Yes, but—'

'We can only deal with this short-term at the moment,' the older woman cut in. 'Would you like me to come and stay with you so that we can talk about what's best to do later?'

'But you're going on holiday in a couple of days.'

'I can quite easily put that off.'

But Lucie knew that this was a trip to South America that her aunt had set her heart on and had been saving up to pay for for ages. 'No, I can't possibly let you do that. But I would like to come over and spend the day with you tomorrow, if that's OK.'

'Of course it is. Will you bring Sam with you or leave him with your mother-in-law?'

'I'll bring him.'

'Then drive very carefully. And don't let this phone call upset you too much. We'll deal with it. He'll be stopped. I'll see you tomorrow, in time for lunch.'

Lucie replaced the receiver, then immediately took it off again, afraid that Rick might be trying to call. But Seton would be calling too, later on, as he rang every night when he was away from home. Sometimes he called early, to catch Sam, but more often he rang later when he knew she would be in bed, so that their conversation was loving, intimate. Luckily she had a mobile phone that she used whenever she went out in the car, so Lucie found it and turned it on. If Seton couldn't get through on the permanent line then he would undoubtedly try the mobile.

Which he did, about ten-thirty that evening. Only, Lucie wasn't in bed but in the sitting-room, the curtains closed, the lights and lamps on, and all the doors and windows securely bolted. This intrusion into her life had immediately killed her sense of security, and she was hating being alone.

'Hello, darling,' Seton greeted her. 'Did you know that Sam has been playing with the phone again and left one off the hook?'

'Seton.' There was an ache and longing in her voice, a desperate need for his strength and comfort, but Lucie bit her lip, knowing that she must try to hide it.

But her husband knew every nuance of her voice and immediately sensed that something was wrong. 'What is it?' he demanded sharply.

'I left the phone off on purpose. I—I had some nuisance calls.'

'A heavy breather, you mean?'

'Yes.' She clutched at the idea. 'So I left the phone off.'

'Damn the man!' Seton cursed. 'Did you try to trace the call?'

'Yes, but he'd pre-dialled to prevent it,' Lucie improvised, angry for not having thought of that herself.

'If only I'd been there. You should have rung me so that I could have come home.'

'Drive all that way, and back again tomorrow, just because of some stupid pervert? Of course not. I'm all right. Really.' Lucie tried to make her voice convincing, not wanting him to worry. 'But I've decided to have the number changed. They're going to see to it tomorrow. And—and I've asked them to make it ex-directory. I'm sorry, I know it's a nuisance but—'

'Of course not,' Seton cut in. 'I would have suggested it myself.'

She gave an audible sigh of relief and, because she knew it was safe to do so, Lucie was able to make a token protest. 'But your agent and your office?'

'I'll give them the new number, of course, but letting friends and business colleagues know is far different from having it printed in a directory for every damn nutcase to read.' Seton's voice was still angry; he was frustrated at not being with her. 'Are you sure you're all right, darling? Shall I ask my parents to come round and keep you company?'

'At this time of night? No, of course I'm all right. It was just a bit unnerving that's all. I'm fine. But I did phone Aunt Kate and I'm going over there for the day tomorrow, to help her pack for her holiday. And by the time I get back the number will be changed so everything will be OK, won't it?'

'I wish I was with you,' Seton said again.

'Well, so do I, but for a much better reason than that.' Lucie made her voice flirtatious, wanting to distract him.

Seton laughed. 'Are you in bed?'

'Yes,' she lied.

'What are you wearing?'

'The cream silk nightdress you bought me for my birthday. You remember?'

'Very well.' He gave a deep sigh that was almost a groan. 'Lord, Lucie, you turn me on just thinking about you.'

'Good.' She kept her voice husky. 'In that case you'll be even more frustrated when you come home.'

They talked for another ten minutes, Lucie taking great comfort from just hearing his voice. Going upstairs, she looked in on Sam, who had, as usual, kicked off his duvet. She covered him up again, careful not to wake him, but then couldn't resist reaching out to touch his hand.

Still asleep, he curled his hand round her finger and held it tightly. A great surge of love for him filled her heart—a love that was different from that she felt for Seton but equally strong. It was a fierce, protective love, this maternal instinct, and Lucie knew that she would do everything within her power not to let Sam be hurt. Or Seton, if it came to that. That was why she had never told him the truth, and now she must never let him know that she had once been branded a thief and put into prison.

Lucie sat by Sam's bed for a long time, just looking down at her child, but when she eventually went to bed she was too tormented to sleep. If only that photograph hadn't been printed in the paper, or Fiona hadn't given their names. But her friends had thought it harmless, had enjoyed their brief moment of fame, because their lives were all clear and open; no dark secrets hid in their pasts just waiting to emerge and ruin their futures.

Angrily Lucie sat up and turned on the light, furious with the fate that had dealt her such a blow. But surely Rick wouldn't be able to phone her again once her number had been changed? She tried hard to be optimistic, but Lucie was haunted by the thought of what might happen. He knew her married name and where she lived. Even if they moved away he would probably be able to find her, because if Seton got elected to parliament then he would be a public figure and easily traced.

Lucie was certain he would be elected; she had supreme faith and confidence in his abilities to do any job he chose, and she was sure that the electors would see the same qualities in him as she did. He would make a wonderful MP, and nothing must happen to spoil that, which meant, yet again, that her secret must never be told.

Feeling far from optimistic, Lucie slept at last, and, the next day, drove up to the cottage in Derbyshire to which Aunt Kate had retired. It was a long journey but the sports car Seton had bought her, red and sleek and great fun, ate up the miles. She was glad, though, when she finally got there.

Waiting until Sam had run into the garden to look at the horses in a neighbouring field and was out of earshot, Lucie told her aunt of her fears, but Aunt Kate said, 'You know what I think is the best thing to do, don't you?'

'Yes,' Lucie agreed wearily. 'But I can't tell them.'

'Them?'

Lucie turned to look fully at her, her eyes desolate. 'Seton—and Sam.'

'Sam?' Kate Brownlow frowned. 'But he's just a child! You needn't tell him.'

Patiently Lucie explained. 'If Seton knows the truth then he will feel honour bound to withdraw as a candidate. But his parents are so proud that he's been selected. They would be terribly upset, and would have to be told the reason why. They would try to understand but they would hate me for it; I just know they would. They're so ambitious for Seton. And one day they would tell Sam, because he would want to know why his father had given up a promising career in politics even before it really got started.'

'But surely...?' Kate paused, then gave a reluctant nod. 'I see what you mean; if you tell Seton then, one day, you would have to tell Sam too.'

'Yes.'

'It might still be better to tell Seton now, get it over with,' her aunt said with a contemplative look in her eyes.

Recognising it, Lucie said fiercely. 'No, never!' She raised determined eyes to this woman she had come to love. 'And if you go behind my back and tell him then—then I'll never speak to you again.'

Her aunt stared. 'Oh, Lucie!'

'I'm sorry, but you have to know how deeply I feel about this. I've never cared more about anything in my life, and I'll do *anything* to prevent Seton from learning the truth.'

When she reached home that evening, Lucie was relieved to find that the phone company had kept their promise and the number had been changed. Inevitably it was to cause some inconvenience and they were to receive a few irate letters from people who hadn't been able to reach them by phone. Seton, though, when he came home was very good about it, and still angry that she'd been upset. He arrived with a huge bouquet of flowers for her which he only just saved from being crushed as she rushed into his arms.

'Darling!' He dropped the flowers on a table and held her close. 'Why, you're trembling.'

'I'm so glad you're home. So glad.' Lucie clung to him tightly, taking comfort as she always did from his strength, his nearness.

After kissing her, Seton led her into the sitting-room and pulled her down beside him on the settee. His voice harsh with suppressed anger, he said, 'What did that pervert say to you?'

Lucie pushed her hair back with a nervous hand. 'He—he didn't say anything. I put the phone down.' She gave a shaky laugh. 'I'm sorry; you probably think I'm making a great fuss about nothing.'

'Of course not.' But, looking into her face and seeing the dark shadows round her eyes, he said, 'Although it's not like you to get so upset.'

Fear that he might start questioning gripped her, so Lucie managed to say flippantly, 'Must be my interesting condition.'

'Did you go to the doctor's to confirm it?'

'No. I went up to see Aunt Kate, remember?'

'Of course. But there can be no doubt?'

'No.' She smiled at him, but somehow the joy that the knowledge should have given her wasn't in her face.

Seton frowned, unease in his eyes, and pulled her to him. 'It's understandable that you feel nervous here on your own. I'll try to go away as little as possible in the next few months.'

She sat up straight, tried to make her voice firm. 'No, you mustn't do that. I was just being silly, over-reacting. Now the number's been changed I'll be fine. Really. And next week I'll go to see our doctor. Then, when we get the result, we'll tell your parents, shall we?'

That thought distracted him, as she'd hoped it would, and the weekend progressed with some kind of normality. They took Sam to a play-barn the following morning, drinking coffee with some other parents while he enjoyed himself. In the afternoon Seton went to cricket practice while Lucie took Sam to a friend's birthday party, held in the village hall, where the thirty or so children were able to run wild and where Lucie was kept busy helping the distracted mother of the birthday child and so, thankfully, had no time to think.

That evening they went to dinner at the house of friends, on Sunday morning they worked in the garden, and in the afternoon took Sam to the local pool, which he loved. He could already swim well and Seton was teaching him the backstroke. So it wasn't until Sunday night that Lucie and Seton were really alone together.

Lucie tried very hard to be bright and happy, and largely succeeded. When they were in bed she said, 'It's been a busy weekend.' He murmured an acknowledgement, and she added, 'Did you do it on purpose? To take my mind off that phone call?'

Seton chuckled. 'I'm that transparent, am I? But you're not so worried about it now, are you?'

'No.' Lucie tried to sound positive. 'No, of course not.'

'Good.' He kissed her back. 'You looked gorgeous in your swimsuit today.'

'I shall soon be fat.'

Putting his hand on her stomach, Seton said, 'The baby has to grow. And you'll be radiant and lovely, as you were with Sam.' He stroked her gently. 'Do you think it will be a girl?'

'You can tell on the scan sometimes. Do you want me to try and find out?'

'No. Let's wait and then have a lovely surprise.'

'It might not be a girl,' she warned.

'Well, a boy would be absolutely marvellous too— and maybe the next time it will be a girl.'

'The next time!' Lucie exclaimed, and punched him on the shoulder. 'Just how many times are we going to try for this daughter?'

'As long as it takes, of course,' Seton said with a grin. 'And anyway I like you pregnant; you look so beautiful and so happy, as if someone had lit a light inside you.'

She laughed. 'Well, I suppose you have, in a way.

He went on stroking her gently. Lucie turned her head and kissed his throat, letting herself sink in the warm, masculine smell of him, in his closeness, in the strength of his arms. Then she said, her voice muffled, 'Sometimes I miss you so much.'

Raising his hand, he turned her face towards him and stroked her hair, then bent to kiss her. 'Why, darling, you're crying.'

'No, not really. It was just—just love, that's all.'

Smiling tenderly, he kissed her eyes. 'My sweet girl.' Moving over her, he took her gently, moving slowly so that their pleasure was prolonged into a wonderful voyage of discovery, culminating in a golden burst of fulfilled delight that left Lucie physically exhausted. Still held in his arms, she fell immediately asleep.

When Seton left to go away again on Monday Lucie was almost restored to happiness. And determined to stay that way. The incident was over; she could forget Rick and get back to living a normal life again.

Her peace of mind lasted for just two more days. Coming home after taking Sam to his nursery class, she picked the post up from the mat and found a letter addressed to herself, the address handwritten. There were other letters so she got herself a coffee and went into the garden to read them in the sun. The handwritten letter was quite short. It said:

Why bother to change your phone number, Lucie? You should know I'll always find you. Remember the last time we met? In court? I'll never forget it—and I'll make sure you don't either.

She should have realised that he would find out her address. With trembling hands Lucie put the letter back into the envelope. The address was clearly and accurately written. He had found out the number of the house as well as the name of the street, and it had been posted two days ago.

Going inside, Lucie put the letter in the empty grate and burnt it, pushing the poker viciously into the embers. Now what was she going to do? But there was only one thing she could do, and that was ignore it. Sensibly, Lucie told herself that if Rick got no satisfaction from baiting her then he would eventually give up and leave her alone. She tried very hard to convince herself of that, but she began to dread picking up the post or answering the doorbell as she waited with inner terror for the next communication.

But for the next two days there was nothing. Everything was back to normal and Lucie began to feel a little more confident and to look forward to Seton's coming home for the weekend. She was giving a dinner party on Saturday night for some members of the local selection committee—a sort of thank-you for having chosen Seton—so on Friday she was busy shopping and preparing, as well as looking after Sam and sprucing up the house.

The phone in Seton's study gave a couple of rings, then stopped, and she knew it was a fax coming through on its dedicated line. Lucie finished the pavlova she was making, pleased with the way it had turned out, popped it in the fridge, then washed her hands and went to look at what had come through. She tore the sheet off the fax machine, read it, and nearly died. 'Don't think you can escape me. I'll always be able to reach you. By the way, I like your car.'

When Seton came home in the early evening Lucie tried to pretend that nothing had happened, that her nerves weren't shot to pieces, but she was unable to hide it completely, and after kissing her Seton looked at her in concern. 'That wasn't much of a kiss! Is anything the matter?'

'It's been a hectic day, that's all, and I've got a bit of a headache. Do you think you could give Sam his bath while I get dinner?'

'Bath this brat?' Seton swung Sam under his arm, the boy giving a shriek of pleasure. 'I suppose I could manage that.'

He took him upstairs and by the time he came down an hour later, after putting Sam to bed, Lucie had dinner all ready. Usually this time was very precious, when they caught up on all the news while he'd been away, when they would talk and laugh across the table, pledging their love for each other in every glance, in every smile. But tonight, when they sat opposite each other, Lucie felt almost like a stranger. The terrible secret she was hiding somehow set her apart, and she found it difficult even to talk naturally.

She managed to ask him how his week had gone, and Seton began to tell her about the hotel where he'd stayed with a couple of other barristers, two of whom Lucie knew. 'Peter Brent has invited us to join them for a weekend at their cottage in Wales,' he told her. 'Evidently there's a lake nearby where they go sailing. It sounds fun. What do you think?'

But Lucie was gazing down at her plate, her fork poised over it, and her thoughts right here instead of in Wales.

'Lucie?' Seton leaned forward and touched her hand. 'Hey, come back to me.'

'What? Oh, sorry.' Lucie managed to laugh. 'I was miles away.'

'So I noticed. What were you thinking about?'

She hastily invented an excuse.

'The—er—the dinner party tomorrow night. I've never cooked for so many people before.'

'You're not nervous about it, are you?'

'A bit, yes.'

'Darling, you have no cause to be. You're a great cook.'

'Thanks, but I don't really know these people, and they're so important.'

'Nonsense. They're just medium fish in a small pond, that's all. Now, wait till I get elected and invite the Prime Minister to dinner,' he joked. 'Only then will you be entitled to feel nervous.'

Lucie gave him the smile he wanted. 'Do people ever really invite the Prime Minister to dinner?'

'I imagine so, but you needn't worry too much; it will probably be a very long time, if ever, before I get on those sorts of terms.'

'You'll be a minister in no time,' Lucie said loyally.

Seton grinned, picked up her hand and kissed it. 'Such optimism—when I haven't even been elected yet.'

'You will be.'

Lucie tried to be cheerful and attentive for the rest of the meal, but a couple of times found herself gazing into space again. She caught herself up guiltily and glanced at Seton. He'd noticed, of course, but didn't say anything until they'd finished the meal. 'Go and sit down and rest,' he suggested. 'I'll clear away and get the coffee.'

'Oh, but you've been working all day and—'

'So have you. Just looking after Sam is a job and a half. Now, do as you're told or I'll put you across my knee.'

Lucie laughed, knowing it to be an empty threat. 'Mmm, I just love it when you get macho.' She hesitated, then said, 'Would you mind if I skipped coffee? I think I'd like to go and have a bath, relax.'

'Of course not. Is your head very bad?'

'It will go.'

'I hope so.' Putting his arms round her waist, Seton drew her to him. 'Because I have been away for a whole week.'

'Missing your oats, huh?'

'But definitely.' He lowered his hands to her hips and held her against his body, moving so that she felt his growing arousal. He had closed his eyes and now let out his breath in an open-mouthed sigh. 'You are the sexiest woman I have ever met.'

'Good.' But instead of kissing him Lucie leaned her head against his shoulder, her eyes on the ground.

Releasing her, Seton said, 'Go on; go and have your bath. I'll be up after I've had a coffee.'

She didn't know how long she had been in the bath, her thoughts full of despondency, but she was still there when Seton came up and had his shower. Afterwards he put on a robe and came over to kneel down beside the bath, where Lucie was staring up at the ceiling.

'Darling, this water is almost cold.'

'Is it? Yes, I suppose I'd better get out.'

She made a half-hearted attempt to rise, but Seton said, 'No, wait. Here.' He turned on the hot tap, then took up the soap and began to wash her. It was something he had done often before and they had both taken delight in it, especially as they knew that it always led to love. Tonight Lucie just lay back and let him do what he wanted, her eyes fixed on his face, trying to fight the misery inside herself.

He glanced at her from time to time and she managed to smile at him, but mostly he was intent on what he was doing, on running his soapy hand along her arms and legs, making patterns where his fingers had lingered. The bubbles gradually disappeared so that he could see her body more clearly. He soaped and caressed her breasts, the flat plane of her stomach, and on down, delighting in the beauty of her slim figure, in every curve of her body, taking extreme pleasure in his task and knowing that she shared it. At length Seton helped her to stand so that he could dry her off. There were a few bubbles on his face where he had been unable to resist bending to kiss her.

Lifting a hand to wipe away the bubbles gently, Lucie said in a voice husky with emotion, 'I love you. I love you so much.'

'Darling!' Wrapping a huge bath sheet round her, Seton scooped her up into his arms and carried her into their bedroom, laid her on the bed. Opening the towel, he began to dry her, but Lucie put her hands on his shoulders, her voice suddenly urgent. 'No. I want you to take me now. Now!' And she tore open the belt of his robe and pulled him on top of her.

Seton gave a gasp of surprise, and his gasps increased in amazement as Lucie almost forced him into her, taking control, taking his love with ferocious hunger, with an abandoned savagery that she had never shown before and which was completely selfish. That it excited Seton beyond control was by the way; Lucie needed him desperately, needed to be as much a part of him as she could possibly be, because only that way could she shut out the fears and the pictures in her mind.

Afterwards, when Seton's hammering heart allowed him to speak, he took her in his arms and said, 'Well! I certainly didn't expect anything like that tonight. If this is what you're like when you have a headache ... Wow!' She gave a perfunctory smile but didn't speak. Stroking her face, he said, 'Was there any reason for it?'

Lucie gave a small shrug. 'I don't know.' She turned her head to look at him, her eyes large and vulnerable in her pale face. 'If I were to lose you I couldn't bear it. I'd want to die.'

He frowned and, because he was so secure in their love, completely mistook her meaning. 'Hey, what's this? Nothing is going to happen to me. Or to you. We're going to grow old and crabby together. We both agreed on that. Now, what's happened to make you afraid?'

She had to give him some excuse, Lucie realised, so she said, 'On the television ...' She didn't have to go on; there was always some item on the television about people dying or being killed.

Tightening his hold, Seton drew her against him. 'You must be feeling tired to let it get to you. Come on, let me finish drying you, then get some sleep.'

But she was already dry so he helped her put on her nightdress and get into bed. 'Would you like a hot drink?'

'No, thanks.' Lucie shook her head and lay back, closing her eyes.

He soon joined her and turned off the lamp, holding her in the way they always slept. Presently, Lucie felt him relax and his breathing become even with sleep. But she didn't sleep herself. With a sick feeling in her heart she was realising how selfish she was being in having another child when all these threats were hanging over her. It was neither right nor fair. The child would be just another victim of her past. The daughter that Seton so wanted might have her whole life blighted by the scandal. For a moment Lucie even wished that she wasn't pregnant. Then, completely appalled by such a terrible thought, she lay and cried silent tears while Seton slept beside her.

The dinner party the following evening wasn't a failure but it wasn't as perfect as Lucie had hoped it would be. She was terribly tired, having hardly slept the night before, and was on tenterhooks all day in case another fax came through. Whenever the phone rang she rushed into Seton's study, but it was always the ordinary phone not the fax. By the evening she felt a nervous wreck, and of course, today of all days, Sam must have sensed her nervousness and played up when it was time to put him to bed. For the first time in his life, Lucie shouted at him to go to sleep.

Seton came rushing into the nursery, his shirt half on. 'What's happening?' Taking in the situation, he picked up a weeping Sam from his bed and said to Lucie, 'Calm down. It's only a few people to dinner. Look, I'll see to Sam while you go and get ready. Is there anything to do downstairs?'

She shook her head, hating herself. 'Sorry, Sam.' Lucie kissed her son, then ran to the bedroom and began to change hurriedly into the clothes she'd decided to wear. When Seton joined her ten minutes later she was almost ready, wearing a simple black dress, her hair drawn back from her head, and the pearl necklace that Seton had given her when Sam was born round her neck. She looked cool, sophisticated and lovely, the perfect wife for a budding MP. Certainly no one looking at her could possibly imagine that only a short time ago she had almost lost control with Sam, or that last night she had taken and given love that was almost savage in its intensity.

'You look fantastic,' Seton reassured her. 'Just relax. They're just ordinary people. If you feel intimidated by them just think of them with no clothes on; that's what my mother used to do when she was first married and had to meet the bosses of Dad's firm.'

Despite herself Lucie laughed. 'How shocking! She never told me that.'

'Hardly surprising. But she assures me it works.'

That incredible idea helped Lucie a great deal during the first part of the evening, when they were all sitting round the dining table, but afterwards the women seemed to go to one side of the room, and the men to the other where they talked politics. All their guests were quite a lot older than her and presumably the women thought that a good enough excuse to ask her questions that Lucie herself would never have asked of anyone, let alone a virtual stranger. After exclaiming over a photograph of Sam, one woman said, 'And do you intend to have many more children, Lucie, my dear? An only child gets so lonely, I always think.'

'Both Seton and I are only children,' Lucie pointed out stiffly.

'Are you? Usually people who have no brothers or sisters tend to go to the other extreme and have large families, I always find. How many do you intend to have?' she probed.

'We haven't discussed it,' Lucie answered coldly.

But the woman wasn't to be put off. 'Haven't you?' she said in surprise. 'I've always told my children that they should decide on what family they want right from the start. So much easier and more convenient nowadays, when you can plan these things. I'd definitely advise you to do the same. It's always best, you know.'

'Really?' Lucie was rapidly becoming tired of what the interfering busybody of a woman always thought, always said and always did. She stood up abruptly. 'Excuse me; I'll refill the coffee-pot.'

In the kitchen, she slammed the kettle down and turned the tap on viciously, getting water on herself in the process. 'Oh, hell!' She switched the kettle on and stood with her head in her hands, trying to calm down, to control herself, to think rationally. OK, the woman was as insensitive and thick-skinned as a rhinoceros, but it wasn't her fault that Lucie wanted to scream against fate, that her life was a mess all over again. Lucie made the coffee and, grimly making herself smile and be charming, telling herself it would soon be over, she took the jug back into the sitting-room.

Their guests must have enjoyed themselves; it was gone one before they finally left, by which time Lucie felt as if the smile was fixed on her face and if they didn't go now—*now!*—she would start throwing things.

She dutifully stood at the door to wave while Seton saw them into their cars, then, immediately the last car door slammed, Lucie ran upstairs and into the bathroom where she started tearing off her clothes, throwing them onto the floor anyhow. Then, the anger suddenly draining away, she leaned against the wall and let the tears silently flow.

'Lucie?' She didn't know how long it was before Seton rapped on the door.

Hastily, trying to make her voice sound normal, she called out, 'I won't be a minute.' She washed her face, taking off the tear-smudged make-up and hopefully hiding the signs that she'd been crying; then she brushed out her hair before gathering up her discarded clothes and going into the bedroom.

Seton had turned on only the bedside lamps and was starting to undress. She paused for a moment in the doorway of the bathroom, the light behind her outlining her body in the silk slip. Seton glanced at her and his gaze held, as always enraptured by her beauty. But then Lucie flicked off the light, dumped her clothes on a chair and opened a drawer to take out jeans and a sweater.

'What do you want those for?'

'To wear while I clear up downstairs.'

Coming over to her, he took them from her. 'It's all done.'

She gazed up at him in distress. 'You've cleared up? Oh, Seton, you didn't have to do that!'

'Nonsense. It took no time at all. Go to bed, sweetheart.'

When they were lying beside each other Seton took her into his arms and began to kiss her. At first Lucie responded, but when he began to pull up her nightdress she turned her head away. 'No, I don't want to.'

'Lucie?' Never before had she denied him love.

She was suddenly and irrationally angry with him, with the surprise in his voice. Why couldn't he see that she was going through hell? Why did he want to go into politics so that she couldn't tell him the truth? And why did he have to put her on this stupid pedestal so that she was terrified of what would happen when the pedestal crumbled and she came tumbling down?

Putting a hand on her breast, he said, 'What is it, darling?'

Still consumed by anger, Lucie pushed his hand away. 'Don't touch me! Leave me alone. I told you. *I don't want to.*' And she swung away from him, lying as far away as she could get.

The startled silence that followed was appalling. Her rage leaving her as quickly as it had come, Lucie realised with heart-sickening dismay what she'd done. Reaching out in the darkness, she found Seton's hand and grasped it. 'I'm sorry. Oh, God, I'm sorry.' And she began to cry again.

Immediately Seton took her into his arms to comfort her. 'What is it, my darling?'

'It—' She was on the verge of telling him every-thing but then lost her nerve. 'It's just that I'm so tired,' she told him, which was true enough.

'My poor girl. I'd never have suggested the dinner party if I'd known it would affect you like this. I'm sorry.'

'It's not that. It's not your fault.' She spoke the words between sobs as he held and tried to comfort her. But Lucie knew with utter despair that Rick Ravena had already sown the first seed of discord into the most precious thing in her life.

CHAPTER FOUR

On Monday morning Anna came back to the house for a coffee after they'd dropped the children off at school. 'Are you all right?' she asked. 'You look quite washed out.'

'Gee, thanks,' Lucie retorted tartly.

In no way put out, Anna said, 'You know I'm on the committee of the tennis club; well, someone's leaving and they need a replacement. I suggested you.'

'No, thanks.'

'But why not? You'd be great. You could take the minutes and things.' Anna waved an airy hand.

'Sorry, Anna, but I don't want to.'

Anna raised her eyebrows at her tone, but said, 'How did the dinner party go? Was it scintillating fun?'

'You're joking! It was gruesome. All the men wanted to do was talk politics the whole time.'

'I can't see Seton allowing that to happen.'

'He tried to steer clear of it, and I tried to get the women to join in some kind of a conversation, but they seemed to be so used to it that they just talked to each other and let the men get on with it.'

Anna wrinkled her nose. 'As you said, gruesome. Have you got to give many dinner parties like that?'

'Lord, I hope not,' Lucie said in heartfelt tones.

'If Seton gets elected you probably will.'

That seemed so far in the future, so distant from her present troubles that Lucie couldn't even envisage

85

it. 'Then I'll deal with it when the time comes—if it ever does.'

'Lucie! It's totally unlike you to be so pessimistic. Have you changed your mind about Seton being an MP already?'

'No. No, of course not.' Lucie managed a smile. 'It was such a terrible evening, that's all.' Suddenly guilty, she added, 'For God's sake don't tell anyone I said that. If it got back to the committee...'

Anna laughed. 'Don't worry. You know you can trust me.' She gave Lucie a contemplative look. 'It might help Seton's chances if you were on the committee of the tennis club, you know.'

Lucie laughed. 'Moral blackmail won't work.' She went into the kitchen to make the coffee and was just pouring it out when the doorbell rang. Immediately Lucie froze, fear filling her heart, then hastily put down the kettle as Anna sang out, 'It's OK, I'll go.'

Lucie ran to stop her but it was too late, Anna had already opened the door. Then Lucie gave a gasp of relief as she saw that the caller held a bouquet of flowers in his hands and she glimpsed the van from the local florist's behind him in the driveway. Going down the hall, she joined Anna in the doorway and took the flowers. They were red roses.

'There's eleven,' the delivery man was careful to point out. 'You're not one short of a dozen; the man who bought them for you specified that there should be eleven. Is it your lucky number, or something?'

'Why, no.' Lucie took them, frowning in puzzlement. She shut the door and took the flowers into the kitchen, Anna following.

'Were you expecting some flowers?' Anna asked, and when Lucie shook her head added, 'How strange to send only eleven. Who are they from?'

Taking out the card Lucie read,

Roses are red,
Violets are blue.
Guess what I'm going to do to you.

There was no name or initial. There didn't need to be. Lucie felt every trace of colour drain from her face.

Anna, reading over her shoulder, gave a surprised laugh. 'Why, that wicked husband of yours! And just what do you think he's going to do—?' She broke off as she saw Lucie's face. 'Lucie?' Her brows drew into a frown. 'They are from Seton, aren't they?'

'What?' Lucie tried to pull herself together. 'Yes, of course.' She gave a laugh that sounded completely false even to her own ears. 'As you say, it's rather naughty of him.'

Anna reached for the card. 'Are you sure? Was there a name?'

But Lucie kept hold of the card and pushed it in the pocket of her jeans. 'He didn't need to sign it. He—er—' She sought desperately for some excuse for the flowers, could only come up with one she was very reluctant to give. She flushed, the colour unnaturally bright in her pale cheeks. 'You see, it's rather a special time for us. I'm—I'm going to have another baby.'

'Lucie, that's wonderful news!' Anna exclaimed, and kissed her on the cheek. 'No wonder you look washed out. I was totally exhausted for the whole nine months when I was expecting Adam. You should have told me; then I wouldn't have pushed you about the tennis club. When is it due?'

'Early next year, I suppose. But I haven't had it confirmed yet, and we haven't told Seton's parents, so please promise you won't say anything for a while.'

'Of course not. But congratulations. And why eleven roses?'

'Eleven?' Lucie flushed again. 'That's—that's rather private.'

Anna laughed delightedly. 'I suppose I can guess. Look, why don't I finish the coffee while you put these gorgeous flowers in water?'

Lucie had no choice but to do so, but she could hardly wait until Anna had left before she grabbed the roses from the vase and one by one, hardly able to bear touching them, shredded them down the waste-disposal. She knew with all too sickening clarity why there were only eleven of them; it had been eleven years since Rick had been sent to prison.

Going quickly to the phone, Lucie rang the florist's number. 'Hello? This is Mrs Wallace. You just delivered some flowers to me... Yes, that's right; he pointed it out. Unfortunately there's no name on the card. Could you tell me if the flowers were ordered over the phone?'

'Oh, no, madam,' the female assistant replied. 'I took the order myself. A man came in and ordered them personally. On Saturday morning, it was.'

'Did he give a name?'

'Well, yes, but I'm not supposed to say.'

'Please. It's important,' Lucie pleaded.

'Well, I suppose it's all right. It was Mr Wallace. He said they were for his wife. He must have thought you'd guess.'

'Yes, I see. I suppose so. Th-thank you.' Numbly Lucie put down the phone, realising it was the sick kind of joke that Rick would enjoy. But worst of all was the knowledge that he had been to a shop only a few miles away to order them.

Lucie collected Sam from school and went home, wishing that she hadn't been forced to tell Anna, who she knew enjoyed relating gossip, that she was pregnant, but she hadn't been able to think of any other excuse. But then she chided herself for getting paranoid; just because one area of her life was turned upside down it didn't mean that anything else had changed.

She began to prepare dinner because Seton was in London and so would be coming home in the evening. They hadn't made love yesterday, although they usually did on Sunday mornings, unless Sam came into bed with them, which he sometimes liked to do. Seton had taken tender care of her, insisting that they go out to lunch so she didn't have to cook, and just kissing her goodnight so that she could go to sleep, which she had done—eventually.

Now she thought that she would probably never sleep peacefully again. The thought crossed her mind that she could go to the police, ask them to protect her from Rick's harassment. They might have done so if she had been what she seemed, a respectable married woman, but she wasn't; she was an ex-con trying to hide her past, and for that reason Lucie was sure the police would merely shrug her off, tell her to sort it out herself.

After putting dinner in the oven to cook, Lucie went upstairs to change, found the card still in her pocket and hastily tossed it in her drawer, then put some make-up on to look good for Seton when he came home, as she always did. But when she looked in the mirror she knew that no amount of make-up was going to help tonight; she looked haggard, her face drawn, with dark circles of tiredness round her eyes.

Staring at her reflection, Lucie tried to think what she was going to do, whether there was anything positive she *could* do, or whether she was just going to have to wait to see what Rick would do next. Lifting her hands to rub her temples, to try to ease the terrible headache, Lucie wondered how long she could go on like this, living such a tormented life.

Eventually she went downstairs and immediately smelt burning. The dinner was over-cooked, completely ruined. Lucie had to throw it away and find something out of the freezer, but it wasn't ready when Seton got home.

Coming into the kitchen, he said, 'Hello, darling. What's the smell?'

He went to kiss her but she rounded on him. 'I burnt the food; that's what the smell is. And dinner isn't ready yet so you'll just have to wait.'

His eyebrows went up at her tone, but he said soothingly, 'Fine. No problem. How about a drink?'

'No, I don't want one.'

'OK. I'll pop up and see Sam.'

'Don't wake him up if he's asleep,' she snapped.

Seton paused in the doorway. 'I've never done so yet,' he said evenly.

She didn't reply and he went upstairs. Lucie was slicing a melon and stood with the knife in her hand, gazing unseeingly down, feeling deeply guilty. Why the hell was she taking this out on Seton? She'd got to pull herself together, not let it affect her like this. If she wasn't careful she was going to harm her marriage—the marriage she so wanted to protect.

So Lucie tried hard to be cheerful over dinner and must have succeeded because she saw Seton, who had been watching her closely, gradually begin to relax. That night they made love, but somehow even that didn't seem the same; she had lost her confidence and with it some of her spontaneity, so that for the first time ever she didn't climax and was glad when it was over. She thought that Seton hadn't noticed, that her own lack of excitement had been lost under his groans of pleasure. But he had, of course.

After he'd rolled off her, he drew her to him and said, 'What is it, Lucie, my love? What's the matter?'

'The matter?' She tried to sound puzzled. 'Why, nothing; I'm fine.' She yawned. 'Tired, though. Goodnight, darling.'

'But it wasn't good for you,' Seton stated.

Lucie went to protest, but then said, 'I'm sorry.'

'Oh, Lucie, I don't want you to apologise! Maybe it's being pregnant. When are you due to see the doctor?'

'Tomorrow morning.'

'Then promise me you'll ask him for something to help.'

'I'm not ill,' she objected.

'Promise me,' Seton persisted.

'Oh, all right.'

But when Lucie went to keep her appointment she didn't mention being tired. What was the point? There was nothing the doctor could give her that would take this terrible burden of secrecy and dread from her.

During that week two more fax messages came from Rick, and also a letter delivered by hand one lunchtime when she was collecting Sam from nursery school. He was, Lucie realised, playing cat and mouse with her. The messages made it clear that he had been watching her; he knew the make and colour of her little red Fiat, said he liked her new hairstyle. The letter referred to Sam. 'Nice little kid you've got. Pity his life is going to be spoilt.'

When Lucie read that she seethed with rage. No one was going to harm her son. No one!

That evening Seton hurried home as he was due to play in the first round of his Draw for a Partner tournament with Anna. His parents came round to baby-sit and they drove to the club. Seton no longer had the Jaguar; he had traded it in for a Range Rover soon after Sam was born as it was so much more convenient.

Lucie sat at the side to watch as the two couples played. It was an indoor court, brightly lit, and as all four players were good there were quite a few spectators. Anna looked good in tennis gear; she was dark-haired so could wear white, and had long legs that she kept always tanned, her little tennis skirt flicking up as she ran around the court.

She and Seton looked to be enjoying themselves; Anna often put her hand on his arm, leaning close as they discussed their game strategy. But then Anna was a tactile sort of person; everyone she liked was treated as an intimate friend, especially men. Lucie knew that, knew that she had nothing to fear, but couldn't prevent a quiver of jealousy running through her.

Anna and Seton won the first set, but lost the second on a tie-break. During the rest period before the last set they sat at the side of the court and Lucie saw Anna lean towards Seton, her head close to his as she said something, a mischievous smile on her face. Seton listened, then stiffened, his eyes searching the spectators till he found Lucie. She smiled encouragingly back, but to her surprise Seton frowned before giving a brief nod. The game started again, but Seton seemed to want the match to end, because he sent powerhouse aces and volleys spinning across the net. Unreturnable, they won the last set in a very short time.

Lucie went to the bar to wait while he showered and changed, but he joined her within just a few minutes, still in his tennis clothes and carrying his sports bag. 'Let's go,' he bit out.

'But I've got you a drink.' She looked at him in surprise, then saw that there was a set look to his chin and knew that something had happened to upset him. 'What is it?'

Taking hold of her elbow, he pulled her to her feet. 'Forget the drink. Come on.'

She went with him to the car and got in as he threw the bag in the back. Lucie looked at him with foreboding, wondering what on earth had happened, but he kept his eyes on the road and was silent, his mouth closed in a grim line. He didn't drive home but took a road that led to open country and turned off into a lane that ended in a local beauty spot, on a high piece of ground overlooking a valley—a beautiful view in the daytime but lost now in the darkness.

Flicking on the overhead light, Seton turned to face her. 'Do you mind telling me why you told Anna you were pregnant when we haven't even told my parents yet, when it hasn't even been confirmed?'

So that was it. Lucie cursed Anna for her indiscretion. 'She wanted me to go on the tennis-club committee,' Lucie explained. 'I said no, but she kept on and on about it. In the end I had to tell her.'

She expected him to understand, to forgive her at once, but his face didn't relax any. Lucie could understand his being annoyed, because they'd agreed to keep it a secret until they knew for sure, but she didn't think that it was such a terrible thing to have done, that it warranted so much anger. It didn't. It was the other thing that Anna had said that had made him angry.

'And what's all this about me sending you red roses with a sexy message?' Seton demanded. 'You don't even like red roses.'

'It was a mistake,' Lucie said hurriedly. 'The florist sent them to the wrong house. I rang them and they came and collected them. They were very apologetic.' She was protesting too much, Lucie knew, but she felt so afraid that she couldn't help it.

Still frowning, Seton said, 'But Anna said the florist asked for you by name.'

Groaning inwardly, Lucie found another lie. 'Yes, that was the mistake; they were for another Mrs Wallace. In the next village. Not for me at all,' she said firmly. Desperately she went from defence to attack. 'Why, what were you thinking?'

Seton gave a short laugh and pushed his hair off his forehead. 'I didn't know what to think,' he admitted. 'It was just so strange that someone had sent you flowers and you'd said nothing about it, that I'd never even *seen* the things at home.'

Lucie managed to give him a pert smile. 'Why, Mr Wallace, I do believe you're jealous!'

'Of course I'm damn well jealous,' he retorted, reaching out for her. 'I know when I'm on to a good thing, and I don't want anyone else trying to take over.'

'As if they could,' Lucie murmured. She put her face against his throat. 'You smell of sweat.'

'Sorry. I was in rather a hurry to find out what it was all about.'

'So I noticed. Idiot. I rather like you all sweaty; it makes me think of cavemen bringing home a dinosaur for dinner.'

'It does, huh?' Reaching up, he turned off the light, then pulled her across his lap. 'I bet you looked lovely when you were little. What a pity you don't have any photographs of yourself when you were young,' he said with true regret. He had undone the buttons of her blouse and pulled aside the strap of her bra so that he could kiss her shoulder.

'I told you, they all got destroyed in a fire.' Which was near enough true. One of her father's girlfriends had once flown into a tantrum of jealousy and had burnt all the photos of Lucie and her mother.

Seton wasn't really listening; he had found her nipple and was gently teasing it into hard awareness. 'When was the last time we made love in the car?'

'Seton! We can't. We're an old married couple. Only people who're desperate do that kind of thing.'

'In that case we definitely have to do it.' He guided her hand to touch him. 'Because I am very, very desperate, my love.'

When they got home Seton told his parents about the baby. They were, of course, over the moon, and stayed for ages, excitedly discussing the news. Seton opened a bottle of champagne and they drank to a successful pregnancy, his mother saying as she lifted her glass to Lucie, 'You've made us so happy, my dear. We couldn't possibly have hoped for a better wife for Seton, for a more perfect daughter-in-law.'

Lucie went over to kiss her, feeling a complete hypocrite, realising that if the truth ever came out it would ruin not only Seton's and Sam's lives but also those of his parents. The new baby's too, probably. There was so much at stake, so much happiness that would be lost.

When they'd gone, Seton said, 'How about drinking the rest of the champagne in bed?'

She laughed and stood up. 'Warm champagne?'

'I'll cool it off in some ice for a few minutes.'

Lucie undressed and got into bed to wait for him. But, as always when she was alone, her mind went feverishly back to Rick and his threats. She realised that his phone call, the fax messages and letters were all part of a programme of victimisation, intended to wear her down and make her afraid. But they had all come to the house when she was alone, so it would seem that Rick's intention wasn't to include Seton in this. Lucie had no idea why, but the thought gave her a little comfort. Her mind began to drift and she turned onto her side. When Seton came up with the champagne a few minutes later, she was already fast asleep.

He teased her about it a few days later as they drove down to spend the weekend with friends at their cottage in Wales. The other couple had three children, the youngest a little older than Sam, and the two days were pretty hectic as they did a lot of sailing, walking and had barbecues in the evenings. Seton wanted to

PLAY
HARLEQUIN'S

LUCKY HEARTS

GAME

AND YOU GET

★ **FREE BOOKS**

★ **A FREE GIFT**

★ **AND MUCH MORE**

TURN THE PAGE AND
DEAL YOURSELF IN

PLAY "LUCKY HEARTS" AND YOU GET ...

★ Exciting Harlequin romance novels—FREE
★ PLUS a Lovely Simulated Pearl Drop Necklace—FREE

THEN CONTINUE YOUR LUCKY STREAK WITH A SWEETHEART OF A DEAL

1. Play Lucky Hearts as instructed on the opposite page.
2. Send back this card and you'll receive brand-new Harlequin Presents® novels. These books have a cover price of $3.50 each, but they are yours to keep absolutely free.
3. There's no catch. You're under no obligation to buy anything. We charge nothing — ZERO — for your first shipment. And you don't have to make any minimum number of purchases — not even one!
4. The fact is thousands of readers enjoy receiving books by mail from the Harlequin Reader Service®. They like the convenience of home delivery…they like getting the best new novels month BEFORE they're available in stores…and they love our discount prices!
5. We hope that after receiving your free books you'll want to remain a subscriber. But the choice is yours — to continue or cancel, anytime at all! So why not take us up on our invitation, with no risk of any kind. You'll be glad you did!

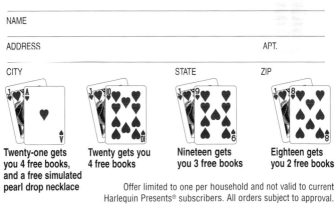

THE HARLEQUIN READER SERVICE®: HERE'S HOW IT WORKS

Accepting free books places you under no obligation to buy anything. You may keep the books and gift and return the shipping statement marked "cancel". If you do not cancel, about a month later we'll send you 6 additional novels, and bill you just $2.90 each plus 25¢ delivery per book and applicable sales tax, if any.* That's the complete price–and compared to cover prices of $3.50 each–quite a bargain! You may cancel at any time, but if you choose to continue, every month we'll send you 6 more books, which you may either purchase at the discount price…or return to us and cancel your subscription.

*Terms and prices subject to change without notice. Sales tax applicable in N.Y.

make love, but Lucie put him off, saying that the walls
were too thin and the others would hear.

'We'll be very quiet,' he urged.

'No, the bed creaks.'

'We could go outside,' he suggested hopefully.

'No. What would they think?'

'They'd think I was a very lucky man.'

'Well, you're not going to be lucky tonight, so go
to sleep.'

'Tyrant,' he complained. 'Wait till I get you home.'

But when they did get home and he made love to
her it was too late. Lucie tried to be receptive, tried
to respond as she had always done, but she was too
tense. There had been a small pile of letters on the
mat and Seton had picked them up and flicked
through them, passing one over to her; the address
had been written in a hand that she recognised.

'One for you.'

Quickly Lucie had slipped it into the pocket of her
jeans and run up the stairs to put Sam to bed, hiding
the letter in a drawer. When she came down Seton
had already gone through his post, and casually said,
'Who was your letter from?'

'Aunt Kate's neighbour,' Lucie lied. 'Just to tell me
that everything at her house is OK.'

Seton raised his eyebrows. 'Don't you usually speak
to her on the phone?'

'She—she enclosed a postcard Aunt Kate had sent
her; she thought I might like to see it,' Lucie
improvised.

There had been no opportunity to read the letter
that evening, but she could think of nothing else, and
certainly couldn't relax now they were making love.

Seton must have felt it. He put his hand on her
face, said her name questioningly. Not wanting him
to think that anything was wrong, Lucie kissed him—
and then, God help her, pretended to feelings that
had always come completely naturally before. She
gasped and cried out as she would have done ordi-
narily, but it was all a sham, an act, done only to keep
him happy.

When it was over, Seton rolled onto his back, then
said, 'Am I losing my touch, Lucie?'

Immediately she knew that he had seen through her,
but, biting her lip, she tried to brazen it out. 'What
a thing to say! Of course not.'

Sitting up, he thumbed the switch on the bedside
lamps, then swung round to look down at her. 'Then
just why did you find it necessary to pretend what
you didn't feel?' There wasn't anger in his tone, but
his voice was full of puzzlement and harsh concern.

Because she felt so wretched about it, Lucie turned
guilt into attack. 'I *wanted* to feel something. Do you
think I didn't? It's not my fault if I couldn't.'

'I didn't say it was. But why pretend?'

'Because I didn't want to spoil it for you, of course.'
Lucie's tone was belligerent. 'Surely you can see that?
But if you don't like it, then next time I won't bother!'

She went to turn onto her side, but Seton put his
hand on her shoulder to hold her still. 'No, Lucie, I
don't like it. If you're too tired to make love or you
just don't feel like it, then OK, I understand and I
accept it, but please don't insult us both by pretending an excitement you don't feel. Can't you see
that such a false act, such a physical lie, belittles what
we have, what has always been wonderful and true
between us?' Putting his arm round her, he lifted her

so that she was leaning her head against his bare shoulder. 'Darling,' he said forcefully, 'even less do I like the fact that you couldn't feel anything. I'm getting worried about you; you just haven't been yourself lately. You must realise it.'

Knowing how insistent, how determined he could be, Lucie began to be afraid and said waspishly, 'All this just because the sex wasn't good enough for you.'

His hand tightened on her arm. 'Since when did it become sex and not love?' he demanded, his voice rough.

Lucie bit her lip, hating herself, and said in a more conciliatory tone, 'Look, I'm sorry. OK? Now can we please go to sleep?'

'No, darling, not yet. We really do have to sort this out.'

'There's nothing to sort out,' she said shortly, and tried to push herself away from him, her hand against his chest. She was in mental torture and desperately sought for a means of escape from his questions. 'Seton, I've had enough of this. I'm not—'

'Perhaps it's being pregnant. Although you were absolutely fine when you were having Sam.'

She grew still, realising that he had handed her an excuse on a plate. It would again mean taking advantage of a lie, of course, but by now Lucie was so despairing that she was ready to grab at any straw. She let out a long breath. 'Oh. Oh, do you think so?'

'It is the only thing that's different, isn't it?'

She nodded, avoiding another outright lie, and said cautiously, 'Being well last time doesn't necessarily mean I'll be the same this time, I suppose. And I— I do feel pretty low.'

'You must go and see the doctor again.'

'I've already seen him once.'

'Then maybe you ought to see a gynaecologist,' Seton suggested.

'Surely that isn't necessary?' Lucie protested. 'I'll probably feel better before too long.'

'But why on earth wait and be miserable when you could get some help and be happy again? If you won't make an appointment to see the doctor, then I will, and I'll take you there myself,' Seton threatened.

Knowing she was beaten, and afraid that he might even insist on going to see the doctor with her, Lucie said stiffly, 'That won't be necessary. I shall phone for an appointment tomorrow.'

'Good.' He kissed her. 'I want you well again, my love.'

Still angry because she'd been pushed into a corner, Lucie pulled away from him. 'Just because the sex wasn't up to standard,' she muttered crossly, and turned her back to him.

Seton didn't say anything but she knew he was watching her. Presently he turned out the lamps and lay down, not attempting to take her into his arms, to sleep as they normally did. For a while they both lay like that, tense in the darkness, then Lucie gave a little sob and swung over to him. Immediately he took her in his arms and held her close, kissed her lips, her eyes. 'My sweet. My little love.' He comforted her as she cried, stroking her hair, her bare back.

'Hold me,' she wept. 'Please hold me. I need you so much.' Lucie clung to him, taking what comfort she could from his physical closeness, and after a while, when her tears had eased a little, she said in passionate despair, 'Promise me you'll never stop loving me.'

Seton held her tighter and said, with distress in his voice, 'Oh, Lucie, as if I ever could.'

'Promise me.' Her voice was fierce, intense in the darkness, and her fingers dug into his arm. 'No matter what happens, promise me you'll never stop loving me.'

'I promise. Of course I promise.' Recognising her desperate need, Seton put his face against hers, felt her tears on his own cheeks and said forcefully, 'I love you with all my heart and nothing will ever change that. *Nothing*, I swear it.'

It was as if his words cast a spell over her. Within seconds Lucie fell deeply asleep, and slept long and dreamlessly.

The alarm clock went off the next morning and Lucie stirred but didn't wake. Seton brought her up a cup of tea just before he left for work, kissed and gently shook her. She spoke to him as he opened the curtains and began to sit up, but when he left she flopped back onto the pillow and went to sleep again. It was a couple of hours later before she woke fully, to find the sun already high in the sky and streaming through the windows. It took a few moments to drag herself out of the almost coma-like sleep back to reality, and then Lucie sat up with a jerk as she realised that it was Monday and Sam should be at nursery school.

Dragging on some clothes, she tore downstairs and found her son sitting in front of the television, the remote control in his hand and his favourite video, that scared him half to death, on the screen. He was sitting in Seton's favourite armchair and had one of their best crystal glasses that had been a wedding present from Seton's parents in his hand.

He gave her a cheeky grin. 'I'm pretending to be Daddy,' he told her.

'So I can see.' Lucie started to smile until she noticed that he had some liquid in the glass. Hastily she took it from him and smelt it. It was Lucozade. The child hadn't, thank God, gone to the length of helping himself to some of Seton's malt whisky to complete his game of pretence. Although he so easily could have done. And it would have been entirely her fault, Lucie realised with horror. She should have been awake and looking after him.

The boy seemed to know what she was thinking. He said, 'Naughty Mummy didn't get up.'

He had copied the deep tones of his father when he was being stern, and sounded so like Seton that Lucie burst out laughing. 'You know what you are? You're a chip off the old block.' Gathering him onto her lap, she gave him a hug.

Sam suffered it with that smugly patient look that every male who tolerates female adoration wears. Recognising it, Lucie ruffled his hair. 'You're starting young, my lad.' She glanced at the clock on the mantelpiece and saw that it was almost ten. 'Do you realise you should be at school? Well, it's too late now, so how about turning off this video and we'll go down to the park?'

He agreed enthusiastically and ran to get ready. Her night's sleep had done Lucie good; she felt better than she had for days, her batteries recharged and more ready to face her problems, but just as they were leaving the phone rang. Immediately Lucie was a bag of nerves. 'Just a minute, Sam.' She rushed into the study in case it was another fax from Rick, but it was the answering machine that clicked on.

Seton's voice filled the room. 'Just called to check that you were all right, darling. Don't forget to make that appointment with the doctor. I'll be home as early as I can. Take care, my love.'

There were several mothers with their children at the swings. Lucie chatted with them for a while but then Sam wanted to sail his boat in the little lake so they walked down there through the trees. It was a lovely day and they strolled hand in hand, Sam carrying the boat, a birthday present from Aunt Kate, under his arm. They passed several people walking their dogs and Sam stopped to stroke the smaller ones. He looked up at her, 'Mummy, can we have a dog?'

'A dog?' She looked at him in surprise, wondering if he needed something to love or just a playmate. 'I don't know, darling. We'll have to talk to Daddy about it. A dog takes a lot of looking after, you know. Have any of your friends got one?'

Sam started to answer her and she concentrated on what he was saying, but as they walked along the tree-lined path she became aware of a cold, creepy feeling stealing over her—a feeling that they were being watched. Lucie shivered uneasily and turned to look over her shoulder.

The path was empty and she could see no one in the trees. Then there was a sudden loud sound of movement nearby. Lucie gave a cry and spun round, but it was only a pigeon flying from a bush. Her heart returned to its rightful place and she chided herself for being silly, but then, with a sick lurch of her stomach, Lucie knew that she had every reason to believe that she was being spied on.

Her gaze swept round in anger now; she was ready to face up to her enemy and do battle, but Sam pulled

at her hand and she realised that there was no way
she could subject her child to the nasty scene that
would follow if she did so. She looked round again,
sure that Rick was hiding somewhere in the trees, but
then let Sam pull her along to the lake.

Sitting on the seat at its edge, keeping a wary eye
on Sam, Lucie remembered the letter that had come
at the weekend. It was still in her pocket and she pulled
it out. When she read the contents it was almost a
relief. Rick wanted money. Five hundred pounds.
Then he promised to leave her alone. He gave her a
week to find it, and would contact her again with in-
structions on where to hand it over.

There were threats in the letter too, of course. He
had found out that Seton had been selected to stand
for parliament, and that no one knew of her past.
These two facts were weapons in his mercenary hands,
swords hanging over her head, knives to twist in her
wounds.

Her hand shaking a little, Lucie tore the letter into
minute scraps and dropped them in the nearest litter
bin. It wouldn't be easy to raise the money, but Seton
paid a generous allowance into a private account for
her to use on the house, Sam and herself. And she
had a little money left over from when she used to
work. Somehow she would manage it.

Because she now knew what to expect, Lucie was
far more relaxed during that week. Another letter
would come at the end of it, she knew, but there were
a few days of respite in which she didn't have to be
afraid of the phone ringing, of being watched by
unseen eyes. When she and Seton made love there was
no need for pretence; she was relaxed enough to be
as receptive and loving as any man could want, losing

herself in his close embrace, in the strength of his body. Perhaps she clung to him a little too much, and when it was over didn't want to let him go.

Seton kissed her deeply, and said with pleasure, 'You're feeling better.'

'Yes, much better.'

'What did the doctor say?'

'Oh, that it was just a stage,' Lucie invented. 'He said I'd probably get morning sickness next.'

'Poor love.'

'It's all right for you, isn't it—being a man?' Lucie said on an envious note. 'You get all the pleasure and I get all the pain and discomfort.'

'Afraid there isn't much I can do about that. But isn't the end product worth it?'

'Yes, of course. Sorry. I was just being feminine.'

'I like you feminine.'

Lucie smiled. 'Well, I have to admit there was quite a lot of pleasure in it for me too.'

The letter came on the following Friday morning, delivered not by the postman but again pushed through the door by hand while she was taking Sam to playschool. It instructed her to take the money at eleven that same morning to a spot out in the more rural area of the neighbourhood, where there was a telephone box with a seat beside it. There she was to sit and wait.

Lucie drove to the place and found it to be in open country towards the top of a hill, with views all round—a perfect spot for such underhand business, she supposed. After parking the car on the grass verge, Lucie went over and sat on the seat. The sun was warm on her back but she felt cold, her nerves on edge. It was so long since she'd seen Rick, when they'd both been escorted from the court after being sentenced. She had been in shock, completely devastated, but she remembered his demonic laughter as they'd taken him to another cell.

Lucie shivered and looked around her, wondering if he was there, watching her, making sure that it wasn't a trap. Then the phone in the nearby booth began to ring. At first she hesitated, then reluctantly got to her feet and went inside, picked up the receiver. Her hand began to shake violently and it was a long moment before she found the courage to hold it to her ear and say, 'Yes?'

'You cut me off the first time I rang you. I didn't like that.' The voice was harsh, vicious, but still recognisable. She didn't speak and he said, 'Apologise, you bitch!'

Strangely, when she heard his voice, a great deal of her nervousness left her. It was something real, solid, and reminded Lucie that he wanted this money as much as she wanted his silence. So she said curtly, 'Do you want this money or don't you?'

Ignoring her, Rick shouted, 'You heard me. You're going to damn well apologise. I'm going to make you lick my boots. Now, say it.'

A flood of anger ran through her and Lucie said acidly, 'I'm sorry you went to prison for nearly murdering that policeman, Rick.'

'That's more like it. I—'

'Yes, I'm sorry you were only put away for eleven years instead of your whole life! In fact I'm sorry that you even exist.'

'Why, you cheap tart; I'll teach you to—'

'Go to hell!'

Lucie went to slam down the receiver but heard him yell, 'Wait!'

After a moment she put it back to her ear. 'Well?'

'You're going to pay for that. How would you like that kid of yours to have a nasty little accident?'

She had a sudden recollection of his casual tolerance of his sister's children, and said, 'You wouldn't hurt a child, Rick.'

'Wouldn't I? How would you know? Maybe not when you knew me before but I've been inside for eleven long years. That changes a man, makes him feel vindictive, especially when he's been shopped by someone he trusted—someone he loved.'

Lucie gave a laugh she didn't recognise as her own. 'Rubbish,' she returned shortly. 'You never loved anyone but yourself in your whole life.'

He swore, viciously, disgustingly. Lucie put down the phone, leaned against the wall, feeling sick. Immediately it rang again, the sound insistent in her ears. Reluctantly, after a long moment of rebellious hesitation, she picked it up and said clearly, 'If you swear at me again you'll never get your money.'

'You want all your posh friends to find out about you, then, do you? Want your husband's party committee to know that you've lied through your teeth to them?'

'That depends on how much you want this money, doesn't it?'

'Bitch!' he swore at her again, then hastily added, 'Don't put the phone down. There's a litter bin beside the seat; leave the money in there. Then go away and come back again in ten minutes.'

'Why?'

'Because I want to count it and check it, that's why.'

'It's all there.'

'Do as you're told and come back in ten minutes, woman,' he ordered. 'Or you'll be sorry.'

Lucie left the money in the bin and drove away; she was in two minds about going back, afraid that Rick might be there, but eventually did so. To her relief there was no one around. Getting out of the car, she sat on the seat again and in a few minutes the phone rang.

'I want your home phone number.'

'No.'

'If you don't give it to me you'll be sorry.'

'Well, I'm not going to so you'll just have to lump it, won't you?'

'And so will you. That was a nice down payment,' Rick said sneeringly. 'Now you know how to do it, you can bring a hundred pounds every week to the same place at the same time. Or else.'

'What? Are you crazy? You said you'd go away and leave me alone.'

'So I lied,' he laughed triumphantly. 'One hundred pounds a week, or you'll see your name plastered all over the papers.'

'You wouldn't dare!'

Rick laughed again. 'You just watch me. But first maybe I'll go and see that husband of yours; I'm sure he'd be interested to hear all about the times we were together, all the little tricks I taught you. Does he enjoy them, Lucie? Does he—?'

Slamming the phone down, she cut off his hateful voice. Oh, God, now what was she going to do?

Driving home, Lucie realised that she should have expected this; having got one comparatively modest payment out of her, Rick was hardly likely to leave it there. She was open to blackmail and he knew it. There would be no end to it.

Lucie saw with horror that it could go on all her life. She must do something, stop him somehow. But the only way she could think of was to go to the police. And they would immediately go to Special Branch and inform them that she was a security risk. Which meant that Seton would be quietly dropped as the next parliamentary candidate and he would never know why. But she would, and she would feel guilty about it for evermore. So which would be worse—to be blackmailed by Rick or to ruin Seton's happiness, his ambition, his life?

It was no contest. Somehow she would have to find enough money to keep Rick quiet. Not as much as he'd asked for, of course—that would be impossible—but enough out of her housekeeping money every week to keep him satisfied.

The first week she left only eighty pounds in the litter bin. Within an hour a fax came through with the usual threats—threats to which Lucie was starting to become immune. She knew that Rick wouldn't do anything while he thought he could still get money out of her. Somehow she managed to keep him at bay for another three weeks or so, but by then had run completely out of money.

When Seton came home one evening, she said as casually as she could, 'Do you think you could let me have some money? The washing machine broke down today and I had to pay the repair man cash, so it's completely cleaned me out.'

Seton's eyebrows rose in surprise. 'Why wouldn't he take a cheque? He usually does.'

'It wasn't the usual man from the village. He's—he's on holiday. So I had to get someone else in a hurry. He would only take cash.'

Seton took his wallet from his pocket. 'How much was it?'

'A hundred and fifty,' Lucie invented, her hands balled into fists under the table. 'He had to replace some parts,' she added desperately when she saw his astonishment.

'That seems an awful lot; the machine isn't that old, is it?'

'I needed it, Seton.'

Handing her the money, he said, 'Yes, of course. But promise me you won't use the man again, darling. He sounds like a cowboy, probably working illegally.'

'OK—promise.'

Lucie took the money with relief, and knew that she was safe for another couple of weeks, but then she was completely devastated as Seton handed her a piece of paper and said, 'The record of all the calls to and from the fax machine came through today, but there are several that were sent here that I don't remember receiving. Do you know anything about them?'

For a moment Lucie's mind was paralysed, too shocked to think of an excuse. Feebly she said, 'Are—are you sure you didn't get them?'

'Quite sure.' Looking at her, seeing the sudden whiteness of her face, Seton began to frown.

Quickly, her voice terse with fear, Lucie said, 'Well, I don't know. I may have received some. Does it matter? We don't have to pay for incoming ones, do we? Is that what you're worried about?'

'No, but I—'

Without waiting for him to finish, Lucie got to her feet. 'I think I hear Sam,' she said, and hurried out of the room, afraid of the astonished, questioning way Seton was looking at her.

By now it was high summer, the playschool had broken up and she took Sam out as much as she could—to get out of the house as much as anything.

Seton was late coming home one night, having gone to an obligatory dinner with the other members of his chambers to mark the end of the session. When he finally arrived, around midnight, he found the house in darkness and Lucie asleep in bed. He undressed in the bathroom and crept into bed as quietly as possible, but Lucie moved, turned over, although she didn't wake.

It was during one of the mini-heatwaves that sometimes hit the country and the night was very warm and humid. Seton lay still, afraid of disturbing her, but Lucie began to toss around, evidently in the grip of a bad dream. She cried out and began to throw her arms around. Quickly Seton caught hold of her and called her name.

'Lucie! Wake up, darling.'

She woke with a shuddering cry of, 'No! No!'

'It's all right, you were only dreaming,' he soothed.

'Was I?' Lucie leaned against him for a minute, trembling from reaction and with the sweat of fear still on her skin. It was Rick who'd caused the nightmare; he often invaded her dreams just as he had invaded her life. A thought occurred to her and Lucie said, 'Did—did I say anything?'

'You called out something.' He added slowly, 'It sounded like a name but I couldn't make it out.'

'Oh. How strange,' Lucie said hollowly, then quickly changed the subject. 'Did you have a good dinner?'

'Very good.' He began to tell her about it but then yawned.

'Go to sleep. Tell me in the morning.'

He nuzzled her neck. 'I'm not *that* tired.'

'Go to sleep.'

Seton chuckled but was almost immediately asleep.

Lucie, though, lay awake and still, facing the terrible possibility that she would say something in her sleep that would make Seton suspicious. It was impossible to go to sleep again, and she felt so hot.

Sliding out of bed, Lucie looked in on Sam then padded downstairs to the kitchen for a cool drink. Even the tiles of the kitchen floor felt warm to her bare feet. She wandered into the sitting-room and pulled open the curtains. It was a beautifully clear night, the full moon lighting the gardens as if it were day. Pulling open the patio doors, Lucie went outside, hoping to cool down, but it was almost as hot outside as it had been in bed, even though she was wearing only a thin cotton nightdress.

The garden was large and completely surrounded the house, and because it was old there were full-grown trees and a high hedge all round that hid it from the nearest neighbours. Sam's paddling pool, an elaborate one with seats at the edges, stood in the shadow of one of the beech trees. The water in it was warm, but Lucie was so hot that she scooped up double handfuls of it and tossed it over her face, feeling the liquid splash onto her cheeks then trickle down her neck and her chest.

Kneeling, she poured the water over her arms, and didn't care that it also soaked the front of her nightdress, making the material cling and become transparent. Getting to her feet, Lucie walked through the garden, threading her way between the bushes and trees, the grass soft under her feet. The church clock chimed one, in the distance an owl hooted and she stopped to listen. Suddenly there was a movement behind her and she swung round, gasping in fright.

'It's all right, it's me.' Seton pushed a branch of the philadelphus aside, the exotic scent of orangeblossom filling the air. 'Couldn't you sleep?'

'No, it's so hot.'

He looked at her figure, silvered and shadowed by the moonlight, and his breath caught in his throat. 'You're so lovely.' Reaching out, he put a hand on her wet breast, caressed it until the nipple hardened, until her eyes closed and she began to pant with desire. Then he let his hand travel down, still caressing her through her nightdress, teasing her into a flame of frustrated hunger, his gaze drinking in the growing passion in her face, glorying in his power to arouse her, in the growing excitement of his own lean, hard body.

When her gasps became moans and she began to writhe beneath his hand, Seton backed her against a tree trunk, then slipped out of his sleeping shorts and took her in a blaze of primeval passion that was joyous both in the taking and the giving, a fit act for the night and the place.

Afterwards he carried her inside and they stood together under a cool shower, Seton supporting her in his arms; then they went back to bed, still wet as they were, because to have dried themselves would only have made them hot again. Lucie slept then, deeply, peacefully, and didn't wake until Seton brought her breakfast in bed the next morning.

She sat up, laughing happily when she found she was naked. Seton bent to kiss her breasts and she let him for a few moments and smiled as she pushed him away. 'I'd better put something on; Sam might come in.'

She went to get up but Seton said, 'No, you stay there. I'll get it.'

He went to her chest of drawers, and pulled open the top drawer to take out a clean nightdress. She saw his shoulders tense, felt his shocked silence. Then he turned with a small piece of paper in his hand and she recognised the card that had come with the roses Rick had sent.

CHAPTER FIVE

FOR a long moment they just stared at each other. Lucie had been too taken by surprise to try and brazen it out and her face was suffused with guilt.

His face very pale, his voice terse with anger, Seton said, 'I take it this is the card that came with the roses you *didn't* receive?'

After a moment Lucie nodded, unable to find her voice.

'They *were* meant for you, weren't they.' Although he phrased it as a question Seton made it a statement, because he had already seen the answer in her face. 'And just why did you find it necessary to lie to me, to tell me that load of rubbish about a mix-up at the florist's?' Seton's tone was so harsh that she flinched; never before had he spoken to her like that.

'I—I forgot to send the card back,' she ventured.

Striding across the room, Seton flung the card on the bed. His voice filled with scorn, he said, 'Don't you dare lie to me, Lucie. Remember, I can easily check it out. Check if my own wife is lying to me,' he added, with the deep bleakness of betrayal.

Lucie couldn't look him in the face. She glanced down, saw that her bare breasts were showing and pulled the covers over herself. She knew that now, if ever, was the time to tell him the whole truth, but the scorn and anger, the disillusionment she'd seen in his face, just at this, made her too afraid to tell him.

'Who were they from, Lucie?' The words came out like a whiplash.

'I don't know! Yes, they were for me,' she admitted desperately, 'but I don't know who they were from. There's no name on the card. Look for yourself.'

'Maybe there didn't need to be a name. Maybe you knew full well without a signature.'

'That isn't true!' With inner wretchedness she tried to make the lie as convincing as she could. 'I didn't know who they were from. I just knew they weren't from you, that you'd never send flowers or a message like that. But Anna was with me when they came and she thought you'd sent them. I didn't know what to do. I threw the flowers away,' she finished placatingly.

Seton stood glaring down at her, the frown deep on his brow. 'Did you phone the florist to see who'd sent them?'

'Yes, but they said it was you.' Lucie was glad that there was one truth in all this.

'It wasn't.'

'I know that. I've just said so. I thought it might be some kind of sick joke. Perhaps even from that phone pest who called,' she added on a note of inspiration.

'So why on earth didn't you tell me?' Seton sat down on the edge of the bed. 'Are you afraid of me, am I such a monster?'

'No, of course not. I didn't want to worry you, that's all. But you do get jealous. You sounded really angry just now.' And, taking refuge in woman's oldest weapon, she started to cry.

Putting his arms round her, Seton kissed her forehead, but said in a voice that was still cool, 'I can't believe that you lied to me, Lucie.'

'I'm sorry,' she said inadequately. 'It just sort of happened. I meant to tell you and then it was too late, and . . .' Her voice tailed off.

'Have you received any other nuisance calls?'

'No,' she assured him, 'there's been nothing since the number was changed.'

'Nothing else has come to the door?'

'No.'

His voice tightened. 'Or on the fax?'

She hesitated for only a second, before giving a definite, 'No.'

But Seton had heard the pause, felt the instant of tension that had run through her before she spoke. Slowly he released her and stood up, his face set. He looked down at her but Lucie avoided his eyes, making a business of straightening the covers. Abruptly he said, 'Eat your breakfast. I'll go and see to Sam.'

Lucie watched him go, relieved that she had got off so lightly but knowing that their marriage would never be quite the same again. Up to this morning Seton had trusted her implicitly, but now there would be reservations. However much he tried to hide it, he would always wonder if she was being completely honest and open. That aspect of it made Lucie feel wretched, but strangely she also felt profound relief; at least she wouldn't have to lie about the flowers again, but she cursed herself for having forgotten the card.

The feeling of relief was short-lived. That week she had to give another dinner party, Sam needed two new pairs of shoes because he'd outgrown all his others, and also he was invited to the birthday party of two of his friends, twins, for whom Lucie had to buy presents. So when she came to find the money for Rick all she could raise was forty-five pounds.

She left it in the usual place and drove straight home—to an empty house because Sam was spending a couple of days with his doting grandparents so that she and Seton could go out to dinner that evening with friends. As she walked into the house Lucie heard the phone ringing. After checking it wasn't a fax, she lifted the receiver. 'Hello.'

'You thought I wouldn't get this number, didn't you?' Rick's voice, full of angry menace, hit her like a blow. 'You stupid bitch, you should know better than that. I'll always be able to reach you, any time I want. Where's the rest of my money?'

'It was all I had,' Lucie protested, knowing it wouldn't do any good.

'Then find it!' He shouted the words at her. 'Sell something. That house is loaded with stuff. I know,' he added venomously, 'because I've looked all round it.'

'No.' Her voice was a horrified whisper.

He laughed. 'I was a burglar, remember? Do you really think I couldn't break into a soft touch like that? I saw the bed you sleep in with that law-abiding husband of yours. What does he think of you having been a thief's cheap tart? Or haven't you told him?' His tone quickened at her silence. 'No, I bet you haven't. I bet he doesn't know.' Rick laughed again. 'I'm going to enjoy telling him all about your shady past. Pity I won't be there to see it, though.'

'If I had the money I'd give it to you,' Lucie said shortly. 'Surely something regularly is better than nothing?'

She tried to be reasonable, but he ignored her, saying sharply, 'I'm getting tired of your games. I'm going to send you a present on the fax, and if you don't pay up the day after tomorrow I'm going to send that same little present to the head of your husband's chambers. And because you've mucked me about and put me to a lot of trouble you can add another two hundred to the payment.'

'But that's impossible! I can't—' She heard the receiver go down at the other end and slowly replaced her own.

The fax came through a few minutes later. It was a copy of a newspaper article written at the time of the trial, giving the whole sorry story and taking it for granted that, because she'd been found guilty by a jury, she must therefore be guilty. The article included a photograph of Lucie, taken at the time, when she was sixteen. The photograph was ten years old, of course, and she'd looked much younger then and her hair had been longer, but anyone seeing it wouldn't fail to know it was her.

Lucie could just imagine the article arriving in Seton's chambers, being passed round for them all to snigger at. It might not get passed any further than that, it might not even harm Seton's political career, but the damage would have been done among his colleagues, who would never have the same respect for him again.

That afternoon Lucie drove into a town where she wasn't known and pawned the pearl necklace that Seton had given her. She would have got more if she'd sold it, but she loved the necklace so much that she just couldn't bear to part with it completely. There was always hope; she might win the lottery or something.

Again she wasn't able to sleep and grew low and dejected. Rick started another campaign of softening her up, more letters, making calls, every one of which contained more threats of exposure unless she paid up. Lucie was able to intercept the letters but one afternoon Seton was home, his case having finished a whole day earlier than expected. When the phone rang Lucie was in the laundry-room and rushed to answer it but Seton got there first. He said the number, repeated it, then slowly put down the receiver. He saw her standing in the doorway and, his face grim, said, 'There was no one on the line. Were you expecting a call?'

'Er—I thought it could be Anna,' Lucie said lamely.

'Really? That's strange—because I saw Anna when I stopped off at the village shop on the way home. She said nothing about having a message for you, or that she intended to phone.'

'It was just a loose arrangement,' Lucie said defensively, but felt her cheeks redden with guilt.

Immediately Seton was at her side. Taking hold of her wrist, he said grimly, 'You're lying! I know you're lying. You were expecting a call from someone else, weren't you? Weren't you?' His voice rose, consumed by anger.

'No! No, I wasn't. Let me go, Seton; you're hurting me.'

But he shook her, yelling, 'My God, I can't believe it! Are you involved with someone else? Damn you, Lucie, tell me!'

'No, I'm not! I swear to you I'm not.'

He stared down at her, his grip hurting her, his eyes filled with tortured doubt. 'How do I know you're telling the truth? How can I believe you? I would have staked my life on you, but now...' Abruptly he let her go, and stepped back. Then he pushed his hair back and strode for the door.

'Where are you going?'

'Out!'

'Where?'

Opening the door, he turned to give her a sneering look. 'What's the matter? Do you want to know how long I'll be out so that you'll be safe to phone him?'

Gripping her hands together in cold despair, Lucie said hollowly, 'There isn't anyone. Please, Seton, don't go like this.'

But he just gave a cold laugh that chilled her to the bone and walked out, slamming the door behind him.

Lucie stared at the door in appalled consternation for several minutes, then ran to it, jerked it open and ran outside. But she was too late; Seton was already gunning the car down the driveway. She shouted but he either didn't hear or chose to ignore her.

Slowly she went back inside, and through the house into the garden, sitting on the seat at the base of the apple tree. Never before had she seen Seton so furiously angry. The thought of his fury chilled her heart, made her hurt inside for having given him the cause. She would have to tell him; there was no other way out. She couldn't let her marriage fall apart like this, not over a foul creep like Rick Ravena.

But what, then, of Seton's hopes of becoming an MP? He would stand down, she just knew; he would think it the only honourable thing to do. With a moan, Lucie put her head in her hands and swayed backwards and forwards, crying with a mixture of tortured despair and indecision.

Seton didn't come home till late that evening. Lucie had cooked a special meal for him and watched it dry up in the oven as she'd waited. She sat on the stairs near the front door, her fists clenched, terrified that he'd had an accident because he'd been so angry, and yet afraid to phone the police to find out in case he hadn't and it embarrassed him.

When she at last heard the car pull up outside she almost fainted in relief and stood up, her face strained as she waited for him to come into the house. Because she had at last made up her mind to tell him everything, and just prayed that his love for her was so strong that he would forgive her.

As soon as he opened the door and stepped inside, she rushed to him, flung her arms round his neck. 'I was so worried about you! I was afraid you'd—' Lucie stopped precipitately as she smelt perfume on him—a perfume she recognised. Then she saw a black hair on his collar and a trace of lipstick on his mouth.

Stepping away from him, she said tautly, 'Where have you been?'

'To the tennis club.'

Her voice hoarse and fiercely sarcastic, she said, 'And I suppose you *just happened* to bump into Anna.'

Seton's eyes, cold and grey as the sea, fixed on her face. 'She was there, yes.'

'And?'

'And what?'

'And what happened between you? Was Martin there?'

'No, she was there alone. She'd walked over.'
Shutting the door, Seton gave her a sardonic look.

'So you gave her a lift home?'

'Yes, as it happens.'

'And did you have to damn well kiss her good-night?' Lucie yelled, her temper suddenly flaring.

'We're supposed to be their friends; I always kiss Anna hello or goodbye, the same way you always kiss Martin. What's the matter?' he bit out jeeringly. 'Don't tell me you're feeling jealous? Surely you should know that what's sauce for the goose is equally good for the gander?'

Lucie went deathly pale, the decision to confess now entirely gone. 'I've told you that there isn't anyone.'

'And there's nothing between me and Anna.' Seton laughed contemptuously. 'Maybe you'll believe me as much as I believe you.'

'Mummy?' Sam appeared at the top of the stairs and Lucie turned to run up to him. When she'd settled him down she found that Seton had already gone to bed. She got in beside him but he didn't take her in his arms. There were only inches between them and yet they were worlds apart.

Somehow they got on with their lives, but again Lucie grew desperate for money. If Aunt Kate had been in the country she would, as a last resort, have gone to her for help, but her aunt was still on her travels, having taken a post teaching English in Peru for six months at a small village school miles from any-where, at a place she could only be reached by letter and then only when a supply plane flew in once a month.

Seton, perhaps in the hope of patching things up, wanted to go away on holiday and Lucie yearned to go, to get away from the pressure and stress for two wonderful weeks. But against that she had to weigh up coming home to a batch of letters and faxes that Seton might find. Full of bitterness, she said, 'I don't really feel well enough to go away abroad.'

'So we'll find somewhere in England,' he said impatiently.

She bit her lip, said, 'I'm so busy at the moment. I don't really think I can find the time to go for a whole fortnight.'

Giving her a bleak look of withering disdain, Seton said, 'Or is it just that you can't bear to be away in case you miss some phone calls, or even some secret meetings? Is that it, Lucie? Are you meeting someone behind my back?'

'I keep telling you I'm not. I'd like to get away, but not for two whole weeks, that's all.'

So they made do with just a few days at the seaside. It wasn't a good holiday; Lucie was too uptight to relax. On their third night there, Seton drew her to him and tried to make love to her. Lucie was grateful that he still wanted her and tried desperately to respond but was so tense that she couldn't. Seton, equally desperate to win her back, terrified that he was losing her, became ever more angry. With a cry of fury he rolled off her. 'Damn you!' he yelled at her. 'I suppose you're wishing it wasn't me, that it was your lover! You'd respond to him, wouldn't you?'

'No, no! It's the baby. I'm afraid you'll hurt the baby.'

'Don't lie! It's months too soon for that. You were never worried about that with Sam. But this baby's special, isn't it? Is that because it's his and not mine?'

Lucie's mouth dropped open as she stared at him; then, lifting her hand, she hit him hard across the face.

The sound of the slap echoed in the sudden silence of the room. A great tremor ran through Seton, not of pain but of despair. Gathering his things, he went into the next-door bedroom to sleep with Sam.

The next morning Lucie was sick and ill, unable to get out of bed, so Seton had to look after her, and because of it they came home early, the holiday that Seton had hoped would bring them back together only having pushed them further apart.

When they got home they were invited to a round of barbecue parties given by their circle of friends. This had become a pleasant habit, each couple taking it in turns to give a party, usually at the weekend. In the past Lucie had always been one of the first to ring round with invitations, but this year she was fervently hoping that the good weather would break before it became her turn, because she just hadn't the money.

Sometimes going to the parties was a relief from her problems, but at other times she felt almost like an alien; she was under such stress that to see people living the normal life she had once enjoyed made her feel like an outsider, someone watching strange people with odd habits like laughing and dancing, having fun. She would find herself standing to one side, watching them, her heart filled with jealousy and something close to resentment.

It was the fourth barbecue that summer. At these parties Lucie and Seton had always naturally gravitated towards Anna and Martin, and automatically did so now. The two women were sitting alone, Lucie gazing pensively into space, trying as always to think of a way of raising some money, when Anna said, 'Hey, are you still there?'

'What?' Lucie came to with a start. 'Oh, sorry. Miles away.'

'You often are these days. Is anything the matter?'

'Oh, no, of course not.' Lucie managed an over-bright smile and began to chat animatedly for a few minutes, but after a while her eyes glazed over and her thoughts turned inward again as Anna replied.

The meal had been a long-drawn-out one, the men doing the cooking but leaving the women to clear up. The children had all gone inside to watch a video and now, as the day sank into a great, golden sunset, their host put on some music and people began to dance. Seton sauntered over and held out his hand to Lucie. 'This is one of our favourites, isn't it?'

'Is it?' She didn't take his hand or get to her feet. The terrible chill between them hadn't melted since they'd been home and, although in her heart Lucie hated it, somehow it seemed easier to deal with every-thing she was going through when Seton left her alone, when she didn't have to pretend to be happy all the time. And she didn't want to dance with him because it would mean his holding her close. He would hold his body against hers and it would turn him on, make him want to make love to her when they got home. But she knew it would only lead to disappointment and frustration again for them both when she was unable to respond, and she didn't dare to try to fake it again.

His voice hardened. 'Don't you want to dance?'

'No.'

She saw his jaw tighten at her curt refusal, at her tone that was little short of rudeness. Then he turned to Anna and gave her a crooked smile. 'Will you take pity on me, Anna?'

The other girl was immediately on her feet, taking his hand and laughing as she went with him onto the lawn. 'Of course—but you're the last person to need pity.'

Lucie watched them go, a weight that felt like solid lead in her heart. She knew that her marriage was breaking apart at the seams but there was at least one ray of hope: in September Sam would go to school full-time and she would be able to get a job for a few months, until she became too pregnant to work. Hopefully it would give her enough money to pay Rick and she would be solvent again; then maybe she would even be able to sleep at nights.

Anna and Seton seemed to be talking a lot; they both glanced in her direction and she knew it was about her. Lucie's flush was hidden by the twilight. She could guess what they were saying. Anna would be asking Seton if there was anything wrong, and Seton... What would Seton say in reply? He wasn't the type to discuss personal problems with others, even close friends, but he had been going through a very trying time lately so he might just unburden himself to Anna, who was certainly looking at him very sympathetically.

Her eyes fixed on them, Lucie saw Anna put a hand on Seton's face and then stroke his neck. That, she thought indignantly, was taking sympathy a bit far. And Seton wasn't being exactly discouraging either. In fact he was smiling down at Anna, his eyes gazing

into hers as he concentrated on something she was
saying to him.

It was a large garden with lots of apple and pear
trees—old trees with thick trunks and low-hanging
branches that were heavy with leaves and created dark
blocks of shadow in the night. The couple danced
away from the main group of people, down among
the trees, disappeared behind them.

Lucie waited for them to appear again, to come
back into the light thrown by the Chinese lanterns
strung across the patio. She waited for ten agonisingly
long minutes but still they didn't appear. Getting to
her feet, Lucie slipped round the edge of the garden,
keeping to the shadows, heedlessly walking over a
flower-bed until she came to the trees. Anna was
wearing white jeans and a red and white blouse so
would be easy to spot, but it took Lucie several
minutes before she came across them.

She rounded a tree trunk and came to an abrupt
stop. The garden backed onto an open field with a
waist-high paddock fence of wooden poles separating
the two. Seton and Anna were leaning against the
fence, their profiles black against the gold of the
setting sun. But they weren't looking at the sunset,
they were turned to face each other. As Lucie watched
in stunned dismay, she saw Anna put her arms round
Seton's neck and lean forward to kiss him.

Lucie waited for her husband to push her best friend
away, and Seton did reach up to grip Anna's arms,
but instead of pushing her away he seemed to be
holding her there because the kiss went on. Unable
to bear it, Lucie turned and ran back towards the
house, blundering blindly into tree branches, hardly
feeling one whip her bare arm. Her heart was filled

with the most terrible despair, but from somewhere she found the sense to slow down as she reached the part of the garden where the others were still dancing.

Seton's jacket was hanging on the back of a chair; she took his bunch of keys from it and then went into the house to find Sam, trying to appear as nonchalant as possible. No way was she going to let anyone know that her heart felt as if it had taken the most devastating blow from which she'd never recover.

Sam was sitting with the other children, their eyes glued to the television screen, and didn't want to leave. Fighting to stay in control, Lucie simply bent down and picked him up, which made him struggle because he was too big for that kind of treatment, especially in front of his friends. But Lucie strode out of the house with him, not saying goodbye to anyone because she just wasn't capable of it.

She drove too fast in her anxiety to get away from that scene of betrayal, kept seeing the picture of them kissing in her mind, but luckily it was only a couple of miles to her own home and she got there safely. As she entered the house, as she saw all the things that she loved, that she and Seton had chosen so carefully, her wretchedness suddenly turned into a great wave of jealousy, an emotion so strong that it completely engulfed her. How *dared* Anna make a play for her husband? *And how dared Seton let her!*

Sam was put to bed with just a washed face instead of a bath, was told off when he started to whine, and was curtly informed that he wasn't having a story read to him and he'd got to go to sleep. Used to his mother being gentle, Sam became silent and just stared at her, but when Lucie firmly turned out the light and closed the door, slow tears ran down his cheeks, the sobs bitten back. Going downstairs, Lucie sat on the settee, her anger growing as yet again she waited for Seton to come home.

It was over an hour later that she heard a car draw up outside and the sound of voices wishing each other goodnight. She had his keys so Seton had to ring the doorbell. Lucie took her time in opening it, the hour she'd spent waiting having increased her anger. She unlocked it and then had to leap back out of the way as Seton sent the door crashing back on its hinges. He stood there for a moment, framed in the doorway, his face a blaze of anger, then he slammed the door shut, took hold of her arm and marched her into the sitting-room.

There he rounded on her. 'What the hell is it with you?' he shouted at her. 'Did you stop to think before you sneaked out of the party and came home?'

Lucie had felt a leap of fear when she'd seen the fury in his face but by now she'd had time to remember her own anger and jealousy and it all came surging back. 'Think about what? What people would say, what they would think? I don't give a damn about that,' she retorted.

'No,' Seton agreed savagely. 'Nor do you care anything about me, it would seem.'

'Why the hell should I?' She shouted the words at him, her face flaming with anger.

He stared at her, for a moment taken aback. His voice suddenly changing from hot fury to cold menace, Seton said, 'And just what is that supposed to mean?'

Her hands balled into tight fists, Lucie said sneeringly, 'Oh, don't try to act the innocent, because it won't work. How long has it been going on?'

His gaze became wary. 'What are you talking about?'

'About your affair with my best friend, of course! And don't try to lie your way out of it, because I saw you together.' Her voice grew raw with pain. 'I saw you kissing her.'

Some of the tension seemed to go out of Seton as he said, 'No, Lucie, you didn't. What you saw—'

'Liar!' She yelled the word at him venomously.

His voice as chill as ice, Seton said, 'I suppose I should be pleased that you care enough about me to be jealous. The way you've been acting lately I've begun to wonder whether you still care for me at all.'

Still shaken, Lucie said, 'Of course I care about you.'

'You have a strange way of showing it.'

'And so do you,' she retorted, some of her anger returning. 'And you haven't answered my question. How long have you been having sex with my best friend?'

Her voice broke a little on the last two words and a contemptuous look came into Seton's eyes. 'Which do you care about most—that I'm being unfaithful or that you're being betrayed by Anna?'

'So it's true, then,' Lucie said hollowly, seeing her life in utter ruin.

Suddenly Seton got angry again. Taking hold of her arm, he shook her. 'No, you silly little fool, it isn't true. Or not my part of it. Although, God knows, some warmth and understanding wouldn't come amiss right now! No, Lucie, I have not been unfaithful to you—not in any way, not even in my thoughts. I made a vow to love you until I die, and no matter what you do I will always keep that vow.' He moved nearer to

her, his eyes, deeply intent, holding hers. 'Because
you are all I want, all I ever wanted. I don't know
what's happening to you, to us, but nothing will ever
change the way I feel about you. Do you understand
that?'

Slowly she nodded, but then her face hardened. 'So
it was Anna, then?'

Seton gave an impatient exclamation and let go her
arm.

'How dare she?' Recalling them together, Lucie also
remembered that Seton hadn't been exactly discouraging. She gave him a hostile look. 'You didn't push
her away.'

'I tried to,' Seton said shortly. 'But she's the clinging
type. I let her know I wasn't interested as soon as I
could without creating a scene.'

That ought to have mollified her, but it didn't; the
jealousy was still there. 'I suppose you enjoyed kissing
her,' Lucie said waspishly.

The look of fury that he'd worn earlier filled Seton's
face again. 'No,' he snarled at her. 'This is the kind
of kissing I enjoy.' And, grabbing her arms, he pulled
her roughly into his embrace, his mouth coming down
to take hers in bruising anger, with a force that bent
her backwards and made her impotent to resist.

She made a sound of protest but it only made him
kiss her more deeply, forcing her mouth open to let
him inside. His hands were hurting her; she felt
powerless and angry. Lucie tried to kick him and he
gave a snarl of rage. Suddenly stooping, he put an
arm under her legs and swept her off her feet.

'No!' She started to struggle, but this man who had
always been so gentle with her, who, before, had
always accepted her denials, just slung her over his

shoulder and made for the stairs. Bunching her hands into fists, Lucie lashed out at his back, thumping him as hard as she could. At one point he staggered a little on the bend of the stairs, but then he recovered and strode into their bedroom, throwing her down onto the bed before he closed the door.

Lucie immediately went to get up but he was back before she was on her feet and tipped her onto the bed again. 'If you think I'm going to let you touch me after you let Anna kiss you then you're crazy! And if you think—'

'I don't give a damn what you think,' Seton spat, and, pushing her down, he came on top of her.

For a while they fought, rolling on the bed, Lucie trying to kick and bite him. But Seton was so much heavier, so strong. She had never realised the power of his strength before because he had never used it against her. But now he laughed when she struggled, his hands easily holding her flailing arms, his body pinning her down. And when he put a hand in her hair to hold still her tossing head so that he could kiss her again, God help her but a wave of excitement went through her, a flame of awareness that she had not felt for weeks.

Again Lucie tried to break free, but it was only token resistance now, and when she went to bite his lip it somehow turned into a return of his kiss and her arms, instead of hitting him, went round his neck to hold him closer.

Their clothes came off anyhow, got torn in their eagerness and were tossed aside. They were not gentle with each other even then; too much had gone before for their lovemaking to be anything but wild and violent. Seton took her as a starved man who had come upon a feast—hastily, greedily satisfying his hunger.

Putting her arms round him, Lucie let him carry her with him, losing herself in physical fulfilment, in the long, spiralling road of rising desire that drowned out all worries and cares, that made her forget everything but the whirling excitement, the sensuous delight that grew from deep within her until it consumed her heart and soul. Her head went back and she gave long, shuddering moans of pleasure, her body arching to hold him, her fingers digging into his shoulders. She felt his body tense as Seton reached his own climax, his breath turn into ragged gasps and his heart hammer in his chest.

Opening her eyes, Lucie, still suffused by the wonder of their lovemaking, raised a languid hand and touched his face. Seton had his head thrown back, taking deep breaths as his body slowly relaxed, and when she touched him he bent his head to look at her. She expected him to smile at her as he always did after they'd made love, to tell her how wonderful she was and how much he loved her. But now his features hardened and there was no tenderness in his face.

Getting up, he went straight into the bathroom and she heard him turn on the shower. Lucie lay there, feeling rejected. Was he still angry with her for having left the party without him? She went over their quarrel in her mind, and it was only then that she remembered what he had said to her downstairs—that he had vowed to love her and he always would, that nothing would ever change that.

With appalled shame, she realised that she had hardly listened to him, that she had been so angry about him and Anna that she had been able to think of nothing else. He had been so serious, so wanting to get through to her, and she had completely ignored him. No wonder Seton had got so mad, and no wonder, too, that he had walked away just now.

Pondering what he'd said, Lucie belatedly saw that that time might even have been right to tell him the truth, all of it, because it was becoming almost impossible to go on carrying this burden alone. Her nerves were close to breaking-point and she felt weak and ill. Really it had all been her own fault tonight. If she hadn't refused to dance with Seton in front of Anna, the other girl wouldn't have taken it into her head to— What excuse would Anna have used to describe it to herself? To comfort him?

For a moment Lucie's heart hardened again, but then she forgot all about Anna as she wondered if she could tell Seton, if she dared. But there was so much at stake, he would have to give up so much. But he still loved her, he had said so, and she needed his strength—the kind of strength he had shown tonight—so desperately.

Getting into bed, Lucie leaned against the headboard, waiting for him. It might not be too late. When he came back she would try to talk to him, lead him again into that mood in which he'd vowed his love for her. And it wouldn't be too difficult, not after the pleasure they'd just shared. Her spirits began to rise as she thought of having this terrible weight taken off her shoulders, and she waited for him eagerly. She heard the bathroom door open but then Seton went downstairs to lock up and turn out the lights. He came upstairs again a few minutes later—but then she heard him go into the guest-room and firmly close the door. He stayed there all the rest of the night.

*   *   *

The school holidays ended and Sam started at a
primary school on the outskirts of the nearest town.
For it he needed a whole new uniform and sports
clothes, books and equipment. It cost the earth. Seton,
more like a cool stranger now, gave her a cheque
towards the cost but it still left her without enough
money to pay Rick the full hundred pounds that week.

Lucie was completely under his thumb again,
thoroughly cowed by fear and perpetual worry, her
only hope that of getting a job as soon as possible.
She could only raise sixty-five pounds, so left that
with a note explaining the situation, saying she'd try
to make up the balance when she could.

For a few days Lucie heard nothing, although she
was on tenterhooks the whole time, expecting every
phone call to be Rick shouting and swearing at her,
making demands she couldn't meet. When she heard
nothing she began to breathe more easily, hoping that
he'd seen sense, that he'd believed her. She drove to
the new school to collect Sam, but found it difficult
to find a parking space, eventually finding a small
gap several hundred yards away that took some ma-
noeuvring into.

Hurrying back to the school, she saw that many of
the children had already come out and several of the
mothers were leaving. Standing with the group of
women inside the gates, Lucie looked anxiously round
and saw with relief that Sam hadn't yet come out.
Anna was there, waiting for Adam; she gave Lucie a
troubled look and seemed about to speak, but Lucie
turned her back on her, not yet having forgiven or
forgotten.

A crowd of children came out and were ferried
away. Adam, who was in the same class as Sam,

emerged clutching a drawing and went off with his mother. The number of children coming out of the school gradually dwindled but there was no sign of Sam. He was probably still chatting to the teacher, Lucie thought with a smile. He had taken to school like a duck to water and was always eager to go. She waited another ten minutes in growing unease; surely the teacher would have sent Sam out to her by now?

No more children appeared so Lucie strode up to the entrance and went inside. Sam's class was at the end of the corridor; she went to it and found his teacher, a girl not much older than herself, tidying up, but there was no sign of Sam.

The teacher smiled at Lucie. 'Can I help you? It's Mrs Wallace, isn't it?'

'Yes. Where's Sam?' Lucie asked anxiously.

'Sam? But he's gone with your husband.'

'Seton?' Lucie stared at her incredulously.

'Yes, he came a little early so that he could take Sam for his dental appointment.'

'But he hasn't got—' Lucie broke off in sudden dread. 'What did he look like?' She got hold of the teacher's arm and shook it, her voice rising hysterically. 'The man who took Sam away—what did he look like?'

'Well, he was tall and dark-haired . . .'

'What else?' Lucie shook the poor woman again.

She frowned, then her eyes widened in triumph. 'I remember now. He had a tattoo on his wrist. An eagle or some other kind of bird. I know I thought at the time that—'

But Lucie was already gone, running out of the school and back to her car, her breath coming in agonised sobs, her heart full of terror for her child.

Her eyes more on the pavements than on the road, Lucie drove along, frantically searching the streets round the school, praying that Rick was on foot, that she would see them. What she would do if she did find them, Lucie didn't even think about; all she knew was that she had never before felt such utter terror, such mind-consuming fear.

'Please let me find him. Please don't let him be hurt.' She was babbling out prayers, tears filling her eyes but being dashed out of the way so that she could see. The fear was like a physical pain and she couldn't think, couldn't reason, knew only that her child was gone and she must find him. But Rick had had plenty of time to take Sam away: she had waited outside too long; she should have gone in as soon as she saw that Sam wasn't waiting for her.

Gripping the steering wheel, Lucie turned into another street and saw a man walking with a child. Putting her foot down, she went tearing along the road and skidded to a stop beside them, narrowly missing a parked car. Both the man and the boy turned round, startled by the scream of brakes, and she saw with sick despair that the man wasn't Rick, that the boy was older than Sam.

She drove on, cars hooting at her angrily when she veered across towards the wrong side of the road, yanked the car into a straight line again, searching, searching. There was no sign of them, but Rick might have had a car; they could be miles away by now. She had to call the police. Lucie was near home, so she sped there, tore into the driveway already starting to open the door.

Sam was sitting on the doorstep.

Lucie shot out of the car and ran to him, took him into her arms. 'Are you all right? Are you all right?' He looked a bit lost and bewildered, but he wasn't crying so he wasn't hurt. 'Oh, Sam! Sam!' She hugged him too tightly in a relief that was almost as overwhelming as the fear had been.

'A man came to take me home from school.' He struggled to get free. 'He brought me in his car but you weren't here. He said I'd got to wait for you.' Sam looked at her accusingly. 'You were a long time.'

Suddenly anger took the place of relief as Lucie set him down and said, 'Why did you go with him? Haven't I told you that you should never go with strangers? Never! Never!'

Sam tried to bite tears back but then began to cry. 'He said he was your friend. He said you sent him. And he gave me this for you.' He searched in his pocket and brought out a letter.

Lucie stared at it for a moment, her face very pale. She could guess the contents but she mechanically tore open the envelope, her hands hardly trembling because she had gone past that now. The note was brief. 'Next time I'll keep him. Bring the money you owe plus an extra hundred the day after tomorrow. If you don't want anything to happen to the kid, then keep quiet and pay up.'

Unlocking the door, Lucie took Sam inside and let him watch television while she made herself a hot drink laced with brandy. She took it into the dining-area that opened off the sitting-room so that she could watch him while she slowly drank it. The torment she'd felt when Sam was lost still haunted her, but it had sharpened her brain, her reasoning, because now she knew that she must think only of him. And she began to think objectively almost for the first time since Rick had started threatening her.

He was, she saw, ruining not only her own and Seton's lives, but now was affecting Sam's too. She couldn't allow that. So she was left with only three alternatives. The first, obviously, was to tell Seton everything. But it wouldn't stop the blackmail; Rick would simply apply pressure to them both. He still had the press cutting with the photograph of her, he still knew everything about her and could sell the story to a newspaper, unless they paid him not to. Seton's career and ambitions would still be in ruins.

It occurred to Lucie that perhaps Rick wanted her to tell Seton because he could get more money out of him than out of her. So telling Seton wouldn't be the end of it, wasn't a solution.

The second alternative would be to go to the police, tell them everything and throw herself on their mercy. Surely if she told them that Rick had kidnapped Sam then they would have to help her? They would find Rick and put him back behind bars. But before they could do that there would have to be a trial, so it would all come out anyway. Again, it was no solution.

Then there was the third way. Lucie didn't have to think much about it; in her heart she knew that it was the only way. And it had to be done now, tonight, because the autumn sessions had begun and Seton was away until the weekend. Picking up the phone, she called her mother-in-law and told another lie, having told so many that she was able to do it quite glibly by now.

'There's been a break-in at Aunt Kate's house. You know she's away? I have to go up there straight away, I'm afraid, so I wondered if you'd mind having Sam?'

She was assured that it was fine, Seton's mother obviously excited at the prospect.

'I may be away for two or three days. I'm not really sure. So could you take him to school? But please make sure that you meet him, that you're there in plenty of time,' Lucie insisted.

'Of course, my dear. He'll be perfectly safe with us.'

After packing some clothes and toys for Sam, Lucie dropped him off at his grandparents'. She hugged him fiercely again when she said goodbye, then had to hurry away, ostensibly to drive to her aunt's house, in reality to hide her anguished face. Back home, she packed a couple of suitcases with her things, then sat down at the desk and wrote a note to Seton. It was extremely short because her hands were shaking and she couldn't keep back the tears.

'I need some time alone. Please don't try to find me. Take care of Sam. Lucie.'

She propped the letter on the hall table where Seton would be sure to see it, then let herself out of her home, her life, her happiness, and drove away to an unknown and unwanted future.

CHAPTER SIX

LUCIE spent that night at Aunt Kate's house. It was late when she got there, almost eleven o'clock—too late to phone her in-laws to see if Sam was all right. But he would be, she knew; he was a gregarious child and enjoyed visiting his grandparents. Would he tell them about Rick collecting him from school? she wondered. It was possible, because he had been taught not to be secretive, but she had been angry with him and he knew that it had been wrong to go with Rick, so he might keep it to himself.

The drive, and all that had happened that day, had made Lucie feel exhausted, but she didn't expect to sleep. But maybe having come to a decision at last, having taken the only step she could to get herself out of Rick's malevolent hold had given her some inner peace, because she fell asleep as soon as she got into Aunt Kate's guest bed, and slept deeply for the first time in ages.

At first, when she woke the next morning, Lucie couldn't think where she was, then she remembered and her heart filled with desolation, and it was then that she cried in heartbroken sobs of anguish for all she'd lost. When her sobs eased a little it occurred to her that it wasn't too late, that she could go back home, destroy her note to Seton and go on with her life. But that life had become intolerable because of the damage it was doing to the two people she loved. She had made her decision and it must be irrevocable.

Now and for always. There must be no going back, no weakness; she had to be strong for Seton's and Sam's sakes. She'd had over five wonderful, perfect years and that must be her only consolation, for the rest of her life.

At just after eight she rang Seton's parents, spoke briefly to Sam, who was fine, and told them that she might have to stay in Derbyshire for several days. 'There are quite a lot of repairs to be done, and the police want me to make an inventory of everything that's been taken,' she told them, dispiritedly extending her earlier story.

They were sympathetic and told her to take her time, trying to hide their pleasure at having Sam to themselves for so long. Putting the phone down, Lucie wondered how they would feel when Seton got home and read her letter and they realised that they would have Sam to look after indefinitely.

Her call over, Lucie turned her attention to her own future. It wasn't a subject that greatly interested her but she would have to do something. It would have been nice just to stay here at Aunt Kate's, but this was the first place Seton would look for her.

That he would look for her, Lucie had no doubt, even though she'd asked him not to. She ought, she thought guiltily, to have made the note more definite, to have said that she would never go back, but she'd hoped that by implying she would return eventually she would gain more time. Seton might not start searching for her if he expected her to come home any day. But one thing was absolutely certain: Seton would never accept just a brief note as an end to their marriage.

So she must move on before he got home and found her letter, find a place where she could lose herself, change her name and just go on existing. Because existing was all it would ever be; her life was over now; there would never again be anything to look forward to.

Taking a road atlas from the bookcase, Lucie looked at it in a desultory way and decided to go to Manchester. It was a huge town where she could easily get lost in the crowds, and wasn't too far away. And there was bound to be a pawnshop there where she could raise money on the rest of her jewellery, her watch, which was a very good one, and the eternity ring that Seton had given her on their fifth wedding anniversary—things she hadn't been able to pawn before because Seton would have noticed.

She thought also of pawning her engagement ring, but found the idea of parting with it unbearable. All she needed was enough money to last until she found a job. And if she couldn't find one right away there was always the car; that was hers, bought for her by Seton, admittedly, but it had been a surprise birthday present so was definitely hers.

Lucie really wanted to keep it, though, because at the back of her mind was always the hope that when she got really desperate she could sneak back to get a glimpse of Sam, and perhaps Seton too, although that would be terribly risky. But she knew that she would have to sell it once the baby came. As yet, probably because of all the stress she'd been going through, Lucie was still slim and the baby didn't show very much, especially when she wore a loose sweater, which she hoped would be a help when she tried to get a job.

Lucie put the thought of Seton's anger, if he ever found her, firmly from her mind and left shortly afterwards, stopping at a roadside café on the way and forcing herself to eat some breakfast, then driving on north-west to Manchester. It wasn't a place she'd been to before and the size of the city overwhelmed her. Where on earth should she start looking for a job, for somewhere to live?

She found herself passing the university buildings and pulled into the side, near a pub. It was open and she went in, found, as she'd guessed she would, that there were several young people who looked like students there, although it was still early in the term. She got chatting to a couple of girls and asked them if they knew of any cheap digs, or where she should go to look, implying that she was a mature student.

They were friendly and helpful, and soon Lucie found herself with a long list of addresses, a pile of change, and a phone booth that she commandeered for the next hour. Most of the places were already full, but eventually she managed to find a bedsit in a house where a student had cancelled only a couple of days earlier. Thankfully Lucie also found a pawnshop, hocked her jewellery, and drove round to the house to look at the room.

It was small and the furniture cheap and basic, but at least it was newly decorated and clean. There was a hand-basin in which she could wash but she would have to share the communal bathroom and kitchen. But just finding somewhere lifted her spirits; after all, when you'd lived in a cramped prison cell for nearly three years then this was paradise in comparison. That it was also the most dreadful comparison to the home she'd just left, Lucie tried not to think about.

So now all she had to do was find a job. Here, too, she was lucky, the fact that she could work at any time and start at once allowing her to take temporary work as a candy-seller at a cinema complex where the permanent assistant had taken sick leave to have an emergency operation. There would be at least six weeks' work and possibly longer.

The hours were unsociable—from two in the afternoon until ten at night, five nights a week—but Lucie didn't mind that in the least. The longer she worked, the less time she would have to think and feel bitter. It was strange, she thought wryly; now that she'd left home, now that nothing really mattered any more luck was coming her way. Maybe the goddesses of fate were trying to tell her that she'd made the right decision in leaving.

The temptation to call her in-laws, to speak to Sam, had to be fought from the first day. Working evenings made it physically easier because that would have been the best time to phone, but the mental torture, the need for her child and to know that he was well, was almost overwhelming. As, too, was her need for Seton.

She missed him every moment of the day, spent most of the time when she wasn't working imagining what he was doing. He would be home by now and would have found her note. How would she feel now that she'd gone? Knowing that their marriage was a mess, he would try to be understanding at first, she supposed, but as time went by and there was no word from her he would become impatient and then angry.

And when that happened he would start searching for her. But she was using a false name and felt safe, secure, both from Seton and Rick. And being safe from Rick was like having a great weight lifted from her shoulders. It was a pity that it had now settled on her heart instead.

Lucie got a half-hour break during her work shift, and took it in the staff rest-room, where she read the paper that she and Seton had always taken. Though tenuous, it was a link with home, and she liked to remember Seton flicking through the pages over breakfast and reading out some item of news that interested or amused him. Looking through it, she would try to guess which items he would have picked out. One night, only her third in Manchester, an item in the personal column caught her eye. 'L, darling, please come home or phone. We love and need you. S & S.'

Lucie stared at it, knowing instinctively that it was meant for her. Her hand went to her mouth and pressed hard against her lips as she tried desperately to restrain sudden tears. She had never thought that he would do anything like this.

Hastily Lucie went out to the ladies' cloakroom. Seton must have been pretty desperate, she realised, staring blindly at her reflection in the mirror. People— their neighbours—would realise that she'd left him; they would see that item and know it was meant for her. Maybe Anna would go round and offer him more 'comfort', she thought bitterly.

Her eyes focused and she looked at her face. She had lost weight, become thin—too thin; her bones showed clearly in her cheeks. But she was fine-boned anyway, so didn't look haggard, just pale and fragile. It was her eyes that gave her away; nothing could disguise their unhappiness, their bleak despair. After that day she didn't buy a paper again.

*   *   *

The cinema complex was on the outskirts of the city, making Lucie glad that she'd kept the car—travelling home so late on buses wouldn't have been pleasant, but in the car it took hardly any time at all. It was a couple of days after she'd seen the ad in the paper when she saw flashing lights in her rear-view mirror as she was driving home after work, and saw that a police car was behind her. Surprised but obedient, she pulled into the side, worried that she might inadvertently have gone through a red light because her mind was elsewhere.

Two policemen in uniform came up, one to each side of the car. She wound down the window and the one her side said, 'Are you the owner of this car, miss?'

'Yes, I am. Have I done something wrong?'

'Do you have the registration certificate for the car?'

'I think so. Somewhere.' Picking up her bag from the passenger seat, Lucie started to search through it.

'Your name, please?' the policeman asked while she was still searching.

'Joan Wilson,' she answered, unthinkingly giving the name she was using. 'Oh, here it is.' She found the certificate and handed it to him.

'And your driving license, please, miss.'

She found that too, and handed it over.

The policeman walked to the front of the car to read them in the light of the headlamps. Coming back, he said, 'You said your name is Joan Wilson?'

'Yes, that's right.' Suddenly she realised where he was heading. Flustered, she said, 'I know that isn't the name on the driving license, but you see—well, I've decided to change my name, but I haven't got round to having the license altered yet.'

'I see.' But he sounded very sceptical. 'It isn't the name on the vehicle registration form either,' he pointed out.

'No, but it's my car.'

'And is another of your names Seton Wallace?' he asked wryly.

'No, that—that's my husband. He bought the car for me.'

'Really? It may interest you to know that this vehicle has been reported as stolen.'

'Stolen!' She stared at him. 'But it couldn't have been. I mean, it's mine.'

'Could you get out of the car, please?' Slowly, reluctantly, she did so. 'I'm arresting you on suspicion of having stolen this car.'

'But you can't!'

But they did, and what followed was a nightmare. They took her back to the police station where she was formally charged and then they put her in a cell. To Lucie it brought back that first time so many years ago all over again. The cell looked exactly the same, it even smelt the same—of disinfectant and fear.

She sat down on the bunk bed, her back stiff, her hands clasped together in her lap, trying not to think of the past, while she waited. She knew what had happened, knew that Seton had reported the car stolen in a desperate bid to find her. And he wasn't to know, of course, just how traumatic being put in a cell was for her, or how she wanted to cringe away from the uniformed men. The whole purpose of her running away was so that he would never find out.

A laugh of bitter self-mockery escaped her; she'd thought she'd been so clever, that she'd disappeared without trace, but Seton had found her so easily, after just a few days. She should have sold the car at once, bought another with the money. But now he had found her and would demand an explanation—and what on earth could she say?

It was the next morning before Seton came. She had stayed quietly in her cell, refusing any breakfast, and didn't look up when the door opened. A policeman, a different one from the man who'd arrested her, said, 'You can come out now.'

Lucie followed him into an office. Seton was there. Lucie glanced at him for the briefest moment, but her heart lurched sickeningly at the scorching look he gave her, in his eyes a mixture of anger and relief, of hope and resentment.

'Do you confirm that this lady is your wife, sir?' a policeman in plain clothes asked him.

'Yes.'

'And do you confirm that you are formally withdrawing the charge against her?'

'Yes.'

'Very well. Here are the keys to your car, sir.'

'Thank you—and thank you again for all your help.'

The policeman nodded and looked at Lucie, not unkindly, as he handed over her bag. 'You're free to go, Mrs Wallace.'

Suddenly she was afraid. Lucie hesitated, looked at the man pleadingly for a moment, but then lowered her head, knowing it wasn't any use.

But Seton had seen and his face hardened. Taking her arm in a grip that hurt, he walked her out of the police station and across to the car. 'Where are you staying?' he demanded curtly, pushing her inside.

She told him, and mechanically gave him directions until they pulled up outside the house. Seton turned to look at her grimly. 'Are you staying there alone?'

'Yes, of course.'

'Give me your keys.'

Silently Lucie handed them over and he took hold of her arm as they went up to her room. The house was silent, empty, all the tenants having gone to work or college. He unlocked the door to her room and gave a small gasp as he saw its stark simplicity, the only ornament the photo of himself and Sam that she'd brought with her. Pushing her inside, he shut the door. Slowly Lucie turned to face him, her chin coming up to take the verbal blows that she knew would rain on her.

'Well?' Seton said bitterly. 'Have you nothing to say, no explanation to give for walking out on us?'

She swallowed, said huskily, 'Please don't do this. Please let me go.'

Striding across the room in sudden rage, Seton caught hold of her shoulders and shook her. 'How dare you say that to me? *How dare you?* Can you imagine what these last days have been like, worried out of my mind, listening to Sam crying for you every night? Can you? *Can you?*' He shook her again. 'Why did you leave us?' She lowered her head, tried to think of something to say, but he put a none too gentle hand under her chin, lifting her face. 'Damn you, Lucie. Look at me.'

Perhaps it wasn't what he meant, but when she did look at him fully she saw that his face was as drawn as her own, the time having taken a terrible toll on him too. There were smudges of sleeplessness and anxiety around his eyes and his mouth was set into a thin line of unhappiness.

It broke her heart. 'I'm sorry,' she whispered. 'I'm so terribly sorry.'

'Sorry!' He almost spat the word at her. 'Is that all you have to say? Well, it isn't enough. I want to know *why*! Why you walked away from us without a word. Is there someone else? You've got to tell me.'

'No.'

'Then for God's sake why? All right, I know that things weren't right between us—but to leave Sam! How could you possibly be so heartless?'

Lucie stood there, unable to answer, her eyes huge in her ashen face. Instead she said with difficulty, 'How is Sam? Is he all right?'

'No, of course he damn well isn't. He misses you terribly and he can't understand why you've left him, why you don't come home.' He had phrased it almost as a question, but again she couldn't answer. With an exclamation he flung himself away from her, then looked round the room. 'Where's your suitcase?'

She began to tremble. 'Why?'

'Because I'm taking you home where you belong, that's why.'

'No! Please, no.'

He had opened the wardrobe, was checking to make sure only her things were there, but swung round to stare at her. 'You're going home.'

Lucie's voice rose. 'No, you can't make me.'

'Oh, can't I?' Coming over, he put his hand on her throat, his eyes filled with such anger and bitterness that she flinched away. 'You're going home and we're going to sort this thing out like civilised people. For Sam's sake. Do you understand?' he demanded harshly, his hand tightening. 'He is the only one that matters now, and I will *not* have his life torn apart. Whatever happens between us I will not let you make him unhappy any longer.'

He glared down at her, his gaze murderous, his breath harsh in his throat. Lucie looked away, closed her eyes for a moment, then slowly nodded, knowing that nothing would stop him.

He seemed reluctant to let her go, his eyes fixed on her face. 'Now, where's your case?'

'Under the bed.'

He brought it out, told her to start packing her things. Lucie did so, packing the photograph carefully so that it wouldn't get broken. Then she went to the bed and took something from under the pillow.

'What's that?' Seton asked sharply. She didn't answer, just held it tightly, so he came to look for himself. 'But that—that's my sweater.' He stared at her in perplexity. 'Why do you have it?'

Lucie shook her head and hastily bundled it in the case, unable to tell him that she held it close to her every night, that she drank in the smell of him that still lingered in its folds. Closing the case, she said stiltedly, 'You shouldn't have come here. You should have let me go.'

It angered him again, but took his mind off the sweater. 'Never!' he said curtly. 'Never like this.' He picked up her case. 'Do you owe anything here?'

She shook her head. 'No.'

'Then let's go.'

But Lucie hesitated. 'I have a job. I ought to tell them.'

'You can do that from home. Come on.' Again he took her arm, as if afraid that even now she might somehow run away from him again.

It was a long drive down to the south and the motorways were heavy with traffic, so Seton had to concentrate all the time. Lucie was glad; she didn't want to have to talk, even to ask more questions about her son. A great feeling of inevitability swept over her; it seemed she wasn't to be allowed to save the people she loved from the results of her past after all. Fate was being cruel, playing games with her, lifting her up one moment and throwing her down to the depths again the next. It just wasn't fair. One mistake when she was young didn't rate all this.

Closing her eyes, she tried to shut everything out, desperately trying not to think of what would happen when they got home. And because she had spent the whole night sitting bolt upright in the police cell, Lucie eventually fell asleep, not even waking when Seton stopped for petrol.

They came off the motorway and Lucie stirred and woke when they stopped at a traffic light. She was resting against the seat with her head turned towards Seton, and when she opened her eyes she found him looking at her. In that moment his face was unguarded, his eyes full of bleak despair, full of the pain of raw hurt and rejection. But when he saw her eyes on him his expression immediately changed, became a cold mask almost of remoteness. Slowly Lucie sat up and turned to look out of the window.

They were on familiar streets now. Seton swept into their driveway and she was thankful that it was screened by bushes; it would have gone all round like wildfire if anyone had seen her being brought home so ignominiously. It seemed strange to walk into the house again, to see all the familiar things that she loved so much. Lucie felt as if she'd been away for years instead of just a few days. Walking in ahead of Seton, she paused to look at a picture, to touch an ornament, her heart filling with pleasure.

After shutting the door, he set down her case and watched her, saw the yearning, the nostalgia in her face. Somehow that hurt more than he could bear. 'Why the hell did you go?' he demanded, the hurt plain in his voice.

Lucie grew still, her hand raised to caress a figurine on the shelf. Slowly she turned to face him. 'I had to.'

'Without even trying to work things out? Had we become so incompatible that we couldn't communicate, couldn't even talk?'

Turning away from him, Lucie took off her coat and walked into the sitting-room. It was clean and tidy—no layers of dust, no scattered toys waiting to be put away. Of Sam, the only sign was a couple of reading books left on the coffee-table. Picking them up, Lucie held them tightly. 'Has your mother been looking after you, after the house?'

'Yes.' Seton's voice hardened. 'Are you implying that someone else might have? Are you still angry about Anna? My God, that isn't what this is all about, is it?'

His voice had filled with rage and Lucie swiftly said to placate him, 'No! Of course not.'

'What, then?'

Lucie pushed up the sleeves of her sweater, feeling suddenly chill, and rubbed her arms. 'I'm sorry, but I can't tell you.'

'What the hell is that supposed to mean?'

'Please don't keep on, Seton. I just can't tell you.'

He rounded on her in sudden, furious anger. 'You disrupt our lives, you drive me mad with worry, and then have the temerity to say that you can't tell me why! My God, Lucie, how can you do this to us? How can you be so cruel?'

'I'm not. I mean—I'm not deliberately trying to hurt you.' She put her hands up to her head and squeezed her fists against her temples. 'Oh, why did you have to follow me? I begged you not to.'

'Did you really expect me to just sit tamely by and let you destroy our lives? You left here without any word of explanation and—'

'I left you a note,' Lucie interrupted.

'The brevity of which was in itself an insult,' Seton bit back at her. 'You didn't even get in touch after you'd left; surely you must have realised how worried I was about you?' Lucie half turned away, not answering, and he gave her a suspicious look. 'I put an advert in the personal column of the paper, hoping that you would see it. Did you?'

Again she didn't speak, but he strode towards her and swung her round to face him. Seeing the guilt in her eyes, he said furiously, 'You did see it!' His face filled with contempt. 'I would never have believed that you could behave so cruelly. Whatever's wrong between us, whatever you think I've done, I don't deserve this from you.'

'Oh, but it isn't anything you've—' Lucie broke off, biting her inner lip. Raising pleading eyes to look at him, she said unsteadily, 'It isn't your fault. Of course not. It's me. I—I needed to get away, to be alone.'

'So why didn't you go to your aunt's house?'

'Because you would have come after me, of course.' A note of anger crept into her voice. 'Because we would have had this—this fight even earlier.' She pushed away from him. 'Do you think I would have left you, left Sam, if I hadn't been absolutely desperate? I *had* to leave. And if you'd thought about it, if you'd thought about me, then you would have respected my wishes and left me alone, not come after me.'

'You must have known I'd look for you.' His eyes raked her face. 'I know that things weren't right, that they had been getting worse for months—but to say that you were desperate! I just don't understand you, Lucie.' Going to her, Seton tried to take hold of her again, but she pushed him away. Exasperated to the point of losing control, he shouted, 'You must tell me what's wrong. You've got to; can't you see that?'

'*I can't!*' It was Lucie's turn to yell. She faced him like a wild thing at bay. 'Damn you, Seton. Just leave me alone.'

He stared at her, his jaw rigid, his hands balled into fists as he strove to contain his fury. Striding over to the drinks tray, Seton poured himself a drink, his hands shaking with anger. 'Do you want one?'

'No. No, thank you.'

Taking a long swallow of the drink seemed to calm him a little. Seton stood with his back to her for over a minute, turning the glass in his fingers. When he faced her again there was a different look in his eyes, speculative, almost calculating. 'The police told me that you were using another name; why use an alias if all you wanted was some space?'

Grateful that his anger seemed to have eased, Lucie said wearily, 'Because I knew it would make it harder for you to find me.'

'So you *did* know that I'd come after you.'

'Yes.' Lucie went to an armchair and sank down into it. She wanted to be alone, to think, to try and work out what to do next. Rick must know that she'd gone away; when she hadn't shown up with his money he would have tried to contact her and would have realised that she'd gone, had escaped him. With any luck he might not come looking for her for a while; she might have a week or so of respite before he found out she was back and started blackmailing her again. Perhaps she might be able to run away again—more successfully this time.

She had closed her eyes momentarily and now opened them to find Seton looming over her, his hands on either arm of the chair. Lucie flinched away, terrified that he might have guessed her thoughts.

But Seton was following a train of thought of his own and said, 'Yes, you must have known that if you'd asked me to give you time alone, if you'd discussed it with me rationally, then I would have done as you asked. You could have gone to your aunt's place and no one would have been so terribly worried about you. You would have talked to Sam as often as you liked, have had the peace that you wanted. You certainly wouldn't have looked as if you were as torn apart as I've been.

'Of course, the objective could have been to make me worry, if you felt jealous or neglected. But you're not the type of woman to act so irrationally, to be cruel for the sake of it—especially not to Sam. So maybe it wasn't me you were running away from.' She gave an involuntary gasp and he immediately pounced. 'Yes, I'm right. Who was it, Lucie? Who were you running from?'

'No one. You're wrong. I'm amazed that you could even—'

Catching hold of her wrist, Seton suddenly yanked her to her feet. 'Don't lie to me! There is someone.' A thought occurred to him and he looked sick. Dragging her with him, he went over to the desk and pulled it open. 'Is it anything to do with these? Well, is it?'

He thrust a bundle of papers into her hands and she slowly looked at them. They were all unsigned but she knew at once they were from Rick. A fax said, 'Nothing came from you today. I shall expect to hear tomorrow.' A letter, addressed to her but which Seton had obviously opened in the hope that it would give a clue to her whereabouts, read, 'Don't hold out on me. Do you want me to come to the house again? Or perhaps I could meet Sam from school for you, like I did before.'

Then there were several messages in Seton's handwriting that he must have noted from the answering machine. Again all the messages were ambiguous, could have been completely innocent, asking her to pick up the phone, not to ignore him. None of them was openly threatening, so Rick must have been careful in case Seton intercepted them.

Lucie tried to be calm, to give nothing away, but what little colour there was in her cheeks drained away, and her hand was shaking as she dropped the messages back on the desk.

'Well? Do you have an explanation for them?' Seton demanded. She began to shake her head and tried to move away, but he jerked her back. His face very bleak, Seton said, 'Who are they from?'

'There—there's no name, so how should I know?' Then she gave a sharp little cry of pain as his grip on her wrist tightened fiercely.

'You cowardly little liar! They're from the same man who sent you the flowers. You've met someone else. Been having an affair. You've been seeing him for weeks, months, ever since you started behaving so strangely.' His face and voice filled with the deepest torment and he suddenly dropped her hand as if he couldn't bear to touch her.

'But it's not—'

'Don't lie! Don't insult me by telling more damn lies.' Seton's face was drawn into a snarl of bitter anguish. 'But you've been lying to me all along, haven't you? Telling lies, living them. Making me think you were ill when all the time you were—' He broke off because the words were too terrible to say, picked up the glass and flung it across the room.

'Oh, Seton, don't, please.' Tears began to run down her cheeks because Lucie couldn't bear to see him so hurt. 'Please,' she begged, and tried to catch his arm.

But he threw her off, seemed to take control of himself by a supreme effort of will, and when he turned to face her again his eyes were full of cold, implacable rage and contempt. 'Have you been to bed with this man? Have you?'

She stared at him, taken aback, not knowing what to say, but he read the answer in her silence. 'I see.' Then Seton laughed. A harsh sound far worse than his hot rage, it pierced her heart, broke it into pieces.

'But you ran away from him too. Why was that, Lucie? Couldn't you make up your mind between us, was that it? Was it too difficult to decide which man you wanted in your bed?'

He flinched at his own words, self-inflicted wounds. 'Or maybe your conscience was getting to you—was it guilt that drove you away? What a coward you are,' he said with another derisive laugh. 'Too afraid to tell me the truth, too afraid to commit yourself to someone else. No wonder you ran away; it was the easy way out for you, wasn't it? And you didn't give a damn about the hell you were putting us all through. God, I could almost feel sorry for this man, whoever he is, if he really cares for you. If you weren't just a cheap lay.'

Lucie reeled as if he'd struck her. She turned blindly away, groped for the back of a chair and gripped it tightly. Seton was right that there was another man in her life and right that it had been guilt that had driven her away, but oh, so completely wrong about everything else. But it was over now; he had ended it himself, because he would never want her back, not after this.

She had tried to run away but now Seton wouldn't be able to wait to kick her out; he would get a divorce and she would never see him again. What she had tried so feebly to do he would now make sure of. So she ought to be glad; he would be able to build a new life for himself and Sam, find a new wife to love him and be Sam's mother. There would be no scandal, no disgrace. Seton would be able to do everything he wanted, go all the way to the top, if he was lucky.

And that was what she wanted too, wasn't it? It was tragic that he'd found her and they'd had to go through this, but otherwise nothing had changed. He and Sam would be free of all the years of unhappiness she would bring them if she stayed. So why did she feel as if she'd died inside, as if she couldn't bear to take another breath? But it wasn't done yet; she must make sure that she killed any feelings he might have left for her once and for all.

So she turned, her chin lifting, and said, 'All right, so now you know. I admit it; I went away to think things through, to decide which one of you I wanted.'

His mouth twisted. 'And do you think you still have a choice?' he said with deep sarcasm.

Trying to ignore that, Lucie said, 'I'd already decided before you found me.' She took a deep breath and avoided looking at Seton. 'I'd decided to leave you permanently and go to him.'

There was a great, heavy silence. Lucie kept her eyes down and bled inside for the hurt she was giving. She loved him so much—so much. When the silence became interminable, Lucie picked up her jacket and put it on, walked out into the hall and picked up her case. She'd actually got the door open when Seton ran up behind her and slammed it shut.

'Where the hell do you think you're going?'

'You won't want me here now. I'll go and—'

'No!' He shouted the word at her violently, his eyes so murderous that she thought he was going to hit her. 'I brought you back for Sam's sake as much as mine, and you're going to stay here until he's happy again, until we can sort out this mess you've made of our lives without doing him any further harm.'

Lucie turned frightened eyes to him. 'But I can't stay here.' Her voice rose. 'Do you hear me? *I can't stay here!*'

Seton's hands reached for her throat, almost as if he would choke off her words, but before he could touch her they were both startled out of themselves as the doorbell rang, loud and strident above their heads. For a moment they just stared at each other, but then the bell rang again long and insistently, and Seton reached past her to open the door.

'Mummy! Mummy!' Sam had been standing on tiptoe to reach the bell, but now he threw himself into her arms and she swung him up, hugging him, laughing and crying at the same time. 'I saw your car. I knew you'd come home.' Sam began to sob. 'Please don't go away again. Please don't go away.'

Lucie kissed him, murmured soft words of love and comfort as she carried him upstairs, leaving Seton to greet his mother who had brought Sam home from school, neither of them noticing a car that had been parked on the other side of the road and now drew away.

It was the next morning when Lucie was in the kitchen with Sam that the phone rang. Sam ran to answer it. 'Hello? Yes, she is. It's for you, Mummy.'

Lucie took the receiver and the voice that haunted all her nightmares said with deep satisfaction, 'So you're back.'

CHAPTER SEVEN

THE previous evening, Lucie had spent as much time as possible with Sam. She had played with him upstairs in his room until Seton had called up that dinner was ready. Afraid that his mother might still be there, Lucie had come down only reluctantly, but then breathed a sigh of relief when she'd seen that they were just the three of them. During their marriage she had come to love her parents-in-law, but couldn't face any recriminations from them now, not even silent looks of reproach.

But his mother had gone and it was Seton who had fixed the meal. Sam, still excited at having her back, was allowed to monopolise the conversation. Seton sat almost silently, his face dark and brooding, only pretending to eat, while Lucie kept her attention on her son and tried to avoid meeting Seton's eyes. After the meal she washed up and found things to do in the kitchen—not that there really was anything; the fridge and cupboards were well stocked and the place was clean; Seton's poor mother had looked after them well.

When she could find no excuse to linger any longer, she went into the sitting-room, where Seton sat in his favourite armchair, his fingers drumming a constant tattoo on the arm, and Sam watched one of his video films. This had always been a good time when Seton was home, this hour after dinner before Sam went to bed, but now Seton shot her a scathing look, knowing that she'd been hiding away in the kitchen, and the air was sharp with tension.

At eight-thirty Seton said, 'Time for bed now, Sam.'

Obediently he switched off his video and came to Lucie. 'You'll come up with me, won't you?'

'Yes, of course.'

She went up to bath him and put him to bed, then stretched out beside him as she had always done to read him a story. But tonight he didn't seem interested although he listened politely, and when she went to leave him he clung to her hand. 'Promise you won't go away again, Mummy. Please promise.' There was such entreaty in his voice, such worry in his little face that her heart filled with dismay. Helplessly, and in deep distress, she said, 'It's very difficult to make a promise like that, Sam.'

He began to cry and she went to gather him to her but he pushed her away. From behind her Seton gave an exclamation and strode into the room, picking Sam up and holding him close. 'Don't worry, old son. I'm here. Don't worry.'

It was, Lucie saw with distress, a scene that must have taken place on the nights while she'd been gone. Getting to her feet, she went to stroke Sam's hair, to kiss him, but he shouted, 'No! Go away!' at her, and buried his head in Seton's neck.

Leaving them together, she went to go into her own bedroom, but realised that she would no longer be welcome there so went into the spare room instead and just sat on the bed. It was some time before Seton came out of Sam's room. Immediately he came to look for her, going first to the bedroom they had shared. He opened the door of the guest-room hurriedly, and visibly relaxed when he saw her there.

'What are you doing in here?'

She raised strained eyes to meet his. 'I'll sleep here.'

He hesitated, then shrugged. 'As you wish. But we have to talk.'

'Not tonight, please. I'm so tired.'

He looked exhausted himself, his face drawn, and thankfully he didn't push it.

Lucie undressed and went to bed, but couldn't sleep. The memory of Sam's rejection haunted her, was the greatest mental anguish she had ever known. She heard Seton go to his room, his step heavy, and wondered if the misery he was going through was anything like her own. A couple of hours later Lucie slipped quietly out of bed and went across the landing to Sam's room. The night-light was on and she saw that he was asleep, still clutching a favourite toy that she thought he'd outgrown ages ago. How insecure the child must have felt to go back to it.

There was a movement behind her and she saw that Seton had followed her. He stood in the doorway, his face set like granite, then said as if the words were torn from him, 'How could you do this to him?'

To both of them, she realised, but Lucie could only shake her head and say, 'I'm sorry.'

She went back to her room and somehow got through the night, getting up early the next morning. She expected Seton to go to his chambers, but he came down in jeans with a sweater over his shirt. Lucie looked at him uncertainly. 'Aren't you going to work?'

'No. I've taken some leave.'

He didn't make a big thing of it but Lucie knew that it must have been hard for him; he was very conscientious in his work and would hate letting his clients or his partners down.

'Would you like some breakfast?' she asked stiltedly.

'I'll get my own.'

'Oh, no, I'll—' She swung round towards the fridge and they collided. Seton automatically put out a hand to steady her and for a moment they were close, their bodies touching. She saw a blaze of emotion in his eyes at the same moment as a tremor of aching need ran through her. The feel of him, the scent of his freshly applied aftershave filled her with almost uncontrollable desire. She wanted him, needed him so much.

'Lucie?' She raised heavy eyelids to find him staring at her and knew that he'd seen and understood.

Quickly she moved away. 'Sorry.' But he caught her arm, his eyes eager with questions as he searched her face. 'Let go of me.' Her voice filled with tension, became abrupt as she tried to recover from her mistake.

But Seton wasn't the kind of man who would let a slip like that pass, and his eyes sharpened. It was Sam who saved her, running into the kitchen to make sure she was still there.

Eating breakfast together was such a normal activity that it got to Lucie and her hands began to shake. She hid it as best she could but knew that Seton was watching her closely. Sam was still in his pyjamas, so she said brightly, 'Shall I help you get ready for school?'

'I don't want to go to school.' Sam thrust his bottom lip forward stubbornly and his eyes had exactly the same look as Seton's when he'd come to collect her from the police station: untrusting and wary.

'Then we'll both have a day off,' Seton said. 'What would you like to do instead?'

Sam looked at Lucie. 'Will Mummy come with us?'

'Of course.' Seton spoke for her.

'Can we go and choose a new video?'

'Yes, but not till this afternoon,' Seton said easily. 'So why don't you go and get dressed and then we'll gather up the leaves in the garden.' When he'd gone Lucie expected the questions to start, but instead Seton stood up and said, 'I've some calls to make and a few letters to write.'

He went into his study and was gone for some time. When Sam came down he seemed to have lost his resentment of the night before and was his usual happy self when Lucie made him some salt dough and they sat together cutting out and colouring shapes to bake in the oven. It was then the phone rang and Sam ran to answer it before Lucie could stop him.

When Rick spoke Lucie couldn't answer, her heart filling with despair that he'd found her after only one day back.

'You thought you'd got away from me, didn't you?' He laughed—a sound that Lucie had come to hate more than anything in the world. 'You're going to pay for that.'

'I don't have enough money—' Lucie began, speaking softly so that Sam wouldn't hear, but Rick interrupted her.

'I'm fed up with the petty few quid I get from you. That's peanuts. Hardly worth the bother. I want some real money,' he said, making Lucie's heart go cold. 'And you're going to help me get some.'

'Help you?'

'Yes. You're coming on a job with me.'

By 'job' she knew that he meant committing a burglary. Her voice filling with appalled horror, she said, 'No! No, I won't.'

Suddenly the receiver was snatched from her hand. Seton said, 'Is it him?' And when she nodded, too taken aback to deny it, he shouted into the receiver, 'Damn you, you bastard. Keep away from my wife!' He slammed the phone down, then said curtly, 'Sam, go and play outside.'

He stood there glaring at her, holding her eyes with the power of his own anger while Sam, sensitive to the tension between them, quickly did as he was told. The second the door closed behind him Seton's hand shot out and grabbed her wrist. 'Were you making plans to leave with him? Were you?' She couldn't speak, but it didn't matter. His face hardened by rage, his jaw thrust forward, Seton bit out, 'Because I'm damn well not going to let you. Did you think I'd let you go without a fight? You're my wife!' His mouth twisted. 'And, God help me, I still love you.'

She stared at him. 'Even—even after this?'

'Yes.' Bleakness came back into his eyes. 'I told myself all last night that I hated you for what you've done to us. I *wanted* to hate you. But I only have to look at you, touch you ...' He looked down at his hand still holding her wrist and raised pain-racked eyes to meet hers. 'And then I know that I can't let you go, that I'll do everything within my power, whatever it takes, to keep you.'

Her silly heart swelling with such joy and gratitude that she thought it would burst out of her chest, Lucie could only say on a tremulous breath, 'Oh, Seton.'

He looked at her for a moment, frowned, seemed about to question her, but then dropped her wrist and stepped away. Lifting a hand, he pushed his hair back from his forehead as he always did when something was worrying him—a gesture so familiar that she wanted to go to him and put her arms around him, let him know that she was there, a part of him. But that was impossible now; she had no right to comfort him when she was the cause of his torment.

Abruptly, he said, 'I'm going to need more time to be with Sam—and to be with you. So I've written this morning to the chairman of the party selection committee, telling him that I no longer wish to stand as their candidate in the next election.'

'Oh, but you can't!' Lucie's face filled with distress. 'You just can't. Not after everything I've been through to—' She broke off, turned and ran into his study. The letter was lying on the desk, ready to be posted. Picking it up, she tore it in half and threw the pieces into the waste basket.

'Lucie!' Coming into the study after her, Seton caught her by the shoulders and turned her to face him. 'Why did you do that? Can't you see that—?'

'Because you want it so much. Because it would be so right for you. And you would be such a good, such an *honest* politician. You mustn't let anything stand in your way, anything! Not me. Not—not this mess.' She shook her head in despair. 'Seton, you *know* how much you want it.'

His hands tightened convulsively on her shoulders. 'But there's nothing I want so much as I want you. Nothing!'

The phone rang again, cutting through the vehemence of his words, distracting them both. Lucie jumped up with sickening fear, her body going rigid. Still holding her, Seton felt it and the bleak, cold mask settled over his face again. Picking up the receiver, he said curtly, 'Hello?' After listening for a moment while Lucie watched him with wide, petrified eyes, he covered the receiver and said, 'It's for me.'

She visibly relaxed, her shoulders sagging with relief, then nodded and left him, not knowing that his eyes were raw with pain as he watched her go. Her thoughts and emotions too chaotic to make any kind of sense, Lucie went into the kitchen and held onto the work surface for several minutes before going out into the garden to look for Sam. He was on the swing that Seton had made for him which hung from a branch of the apple tree, but he wasn't swinging, just sitting there looking at the house, an expression of fear and dread on his small, pale face.

'Want a push?' Lucie asked him.

He shook his head. 'Are you going away again?' His eyes, the exact blue-grey of his father's, were wide and vulnerable.

'Of course not,' Lucie managed to say lightly. 'We're going out to choose a new video later, aren't we?'

'I don't like it when you go away.'

Sitting on the ground beside him, she said, 'I bet you've been having a lovely time with Granny and Grandpa, though. Did they take you to see the new Disney film?'

He let her distract him, but it seemed a long time before Seton came out to join them. Glancing at him under her lashes, Lucie thought he seemed withdrawn, as if he was thinking deeply about something on his mind. But that was understandable in the circumstances, she supposed. 'Who was on the phone?'

'What? Oh—the office.' He didn't enlarge on it but said, 'Why don't we go out to lunch? Sam can choose where.'

'Yes, please. The new burger place.' Sam ran inside to get his coat and they followed more slowly.

As they reached the back door Lucie stopped and looked at Seton anxiously. 'You won't give up the candidacy, will you? Please. Please promise you won't.'

Seton gave her a strange, brooding kind of look. 'I've already done so. I spoke to the chairman on the phone before I wrote to confirm it.'

'Oh, no.' Her face filled with sadness. 'I wouldn't have had this happen for the world.'

His eyes were fixed on her face. 'Wouldn't you?'

'Seton, I'm so sorry, so dreadfully sorry.'

He gave her an odd look. 'Do you trust me, Lucie?'

'Trust you?' She frowned, the question puzzling her, unable to see why he'd asked it. 'Yes, of course I trust you. I suppose you mean trust you to know what's best,' she said gropingly.

But he shook his head. 'No. No, that isn't what I meant—but it doesn't matter.' He turned away. 'Sam's waiting.'

For the whole of that afternoon Seton seemed oddly withdrawn, distant, making Lucie wonder if this was how he was going to behave towards her all the time. Maybe he was regretting that outburst this morning, having second thoughts about wanting to keep her at any price. Before, in the time before Rick had got out of prison and found her, their relationship had always been so open; Seton just wasn't devious, but now Lucie felt that he was keeping something from her. He gave them his superficial attention but there was obviously something on his mind, and his eyes, when he thought Lucie wasn't watching him, kept sweeping round as if he was looking for someone.

It came to her that he might be afraid that Rick—whom he only knew as 'the other man' and with whom he thought she was having an affair—was following them. He hadn't asked her anything personal about Rick—who he was, how she'd met him, that kind of thing. That puzzled Lucie too, until she realised that he probably couldn't bear to know, couldn't stand to hear any details.

After Sam had chosen his video they went to a garden centre where there was a small farm and a miniature railway that Sam loved to ride on, and by the time they got back home they all felt tired. But Sam insisted on watching his video after dinner and only reluctantly went to bed.

Seton stood up. He looked so tired and drawn that Lucie's heart went out to him. 'I'd better go and re-write that letter.'

'Must you? Couldn't you say you've changed your mind?' Lucie pleaded wretchedly. 'Surely it's not too late?'

'On the contrary; I should have done it months ago.' And he walked into his study.

Lucie automatically cleared up the sitting-room and kitchen, and was still there when Seton put his head round the door and said, 'I'm going out to post the letter. I might stop off at the pub on my way back.'

She was surprised that he was leaving her alone, but he would have to leave her some time, she supposed. Pouring herself a coffee, Lucie took it into the sitting-room and sat pensively drinking it. That Seton had decided to give up the candidacy was a terrible blow but also a great relief. At least now if Rick fulfilled his threat to expose her it wouldn't shatter Seton's parliamentary hopes, wouldn't create a national scandal, but it would still be bad enough.

Tiredness overcame her and she decided to go to bed—that cold, lonely bed. But as she got to her feet the phone rang. Instantly she stood frozen with dread. She let it ring and the answering machine in the study cut in. Going into that room, she listened and heard Rick say, 'I know you're there, and I know you're alone, so answer the damn phone or I'll take the kid again.'

With a small, tortured sob, Lucie picked up the phone.

'That's better. Now listen, bitch. I want you and I want your car—the Range Rover.'

'No!'

'Shut up,' he yelled at her, then called her a stream of foul names. 'It's for tomorrow night. You'll meet me at two in the morning where you've been dropping the money off every week. And don't try telling me you can't sneak out, because I know you're not sleeping in the same room as that jumped-up pig of a lawyer.' He laughed richly. 'Kicked you out, did he? Never mind, he'll take you back as soon as he gets randy and wants to—'

'Shut up!' Lucie shouted. 'Just shut up.'

He laughed again, but said, 'I should get enough money out of this job to set me up in Spain. So you'll be rid of me, Lucie. Won't that be nice? And then your kid will be safe. See what happens when you're sensible?'

There was a long silence, then Lucie said slowly, 'Do you mean it? I'll really be free of you.'

'Free as a bird—a gaolbird.' And he guffawed at his own wit. Then his mood suddenly changed. 'And don't try and get clever. If you tell that husband of yours or go to the police, then you can kiss your son goodbye. I won't just take him for a little ride like last time, I'll make sure he's taken abroad, to a place where you'll never find him. And you'll spend the rest of your life wondering where he is, who's got him, and knowing it's all your fault. So be there. All right?'

'Yes,' Lucie answered on a long, tired breath. 'All right.'

She went to bed but it was over an hour later before she heard Seton come home. He didn't come to her room to check that she was there or even call goodnight; perhaps he thought she was asleep, and he must have known that she would never leave Sam alone in the house.

Lucie had no idea how she got through the next day. It was Saturday, so both Sam and Seton were home, but luckily they spent most of the day in the garden, clearing up the leaves and making a bonfire on which they roasted potatoes in the embers. Sam was laughing and happy, his confidence returning, but Lucie watched them both with sad, sombre eyes, knowing what she had to do that night.

At one-thirty in the morning Lucie let herself out of her room and went quietly down the stairs. What preparations she'd thought necessary had already been done: hinges on doors oiled, the petrol in the car checked. The garage doors opened quietly and she let the car coast down the drive and out into the road, letting it roll as far down the hill as it would go before starting the engine. It was very dark, the moon completely obscured, but she knew the way and drove with grim purposefulness. When she reached the telephone box she could see no sign of Rick, but she was early and settled down to wait.

Then the passenger door opened and he slid inside. 'Turn off the courtesy light,' he growled at her. 'Haven't you got any sense?'

But in those few moments she had seen his face and was completely shocked. Once, when she'd known him, he'd been handsome in a dark, saturnine kind of way, but his years in gaol had changed him. His face was fat now, his cheeks swollen so that his eyes were pig-like slits, and his lean jaw had become a pendulous double chin. His hair, which he had once been so proud of and forever combing, had receded, and what was left of it was greasy and unkempt.

He smelt too, of whisky and unwashed clothes and sweat. And of triumph. Taking off a glove, he reached out and ran a hand down her hair and her face, then laughed when she flinched away. Deliberately he put his hand on her breast and fondled her. 'I can do anything I damn well want to you, doll, and you can't do a thing about it.'

From disgust Lucie found courage. 'Not if you want me to help you tonight, you damn well can't!'

He laughed again, but put the glove back on and, taking a torch from his pocket, started to search the car, looking in the glove compartment, feeling under the dashboard and making her get out so he could search under her seat. Then he got in the back, pushed Sam's toys that she'd left there aside, and searched that too.

'Just checking that you haven't taken any ideas into your head about trying to pull a fast one,' he said as he got back into the car beside her. 'Let's get going.'

She started the car. 'Where are we going?'

'I'll direct you.'

They didn't trust each other, which was hardly surprising. Rick gave her directions and occasionally took a swig of whisky from a pocket flask. Twice he tried to put his hand on her leg, but Lucie swerved the car violently, making him swear, and then he left her alone.

He didn't tell her where they were going, but he couldn't hide the road signs, and Lucie took careful note as they drove along. From the trip meter she saw that they'd travelled more than thirty miles when he told her to pull off the road into a narrow, overgrown lane. On one side was a high wall and on the other thick undergrowth. They went along the lane for a couple of hundred yards to a clearing where he made her turn the car round. 'Now reverse down the lane till I tell you to stop,' Rick instructed.

She did so and, when they stopped, found that she was under the outspread branches of a huge tree that grew on the other side of the wall. 'Turn off the engine and the lights.'

He pulled a black Balaclava over his head, immediately transforming himself into a dangerous, fearsome thug. Leaning past her, he took the keys out of the ignition. 'Just to make sure you don't drive away,' he told her. 'And if you do try anything—then so long, Sam. And don't forget—if anything happens to me then I've got friends who'll do it for me.' He put his hand under her chin, gripped her throat till he bruised her skin, enjoying hurting her. 'Do you understand?'

She couldn't speak, only nod. But he was satisfied and let her go.

Getting out, he climbed on the roof of the car and from there got over the wall—using the tree to help him climb down, Lucie supposed. She gave him ten agonisingly long minutes then reached into the back and picked up a toy rabbit of Sam's, pulled a hanging thread so that the stitching in its back came undone and extracted the mobile phone she'd sewn inside. Then she got out and ran back to the main road, following the wall round until she found a gate and the name of the place. It wasn't a private house, it was a club! And a rich and exclusive one by the look of it.

Turning on the phone, Lucie called the police and gave them the address, told them that a robbery was in progress, giving as much detail as she could. When they asked her name she gave it; there was no point in doing otherwise—there would be no escape for her. Rick would surely shop her, and anyway they were using Seton's car.

That massive, irrecoverable step taken, Lucie felt a wonderful sense of relief and concentrated on that, pushing all thoughts of the grim future aside. Walking back to the car, she sat inside it, fatalistically waiting to see what would happen.

After about ten minutes she expected to hear police sirens arriving and got more nervous as the silence of the night was unbroken. Half an hour later Rick came back, jumping down onto the roof of the car, putting something in the back, then breathing heavily as he got in beside her. With a feeling of sick, angry despair, Lucie realised that the police hadn't believed her or had gone to the wrong place. All her careful planning had been in vain. Now what was she going to do?

'Go on, drive.'

'You've got the keys.'

He fished for them in his pocket, gave them to her. As he raised the black sweater he was wearing Lucie caught a glimpse of something metallic and knew that he had a gun. Her blood ran cold, but there was nothing she could do. Starting the car, she drove down the lane to the main road.

The police were there, waiting. They had cars in a half-circle, completely blocking any escape.

Rick gave a gasp of horrified dismay. 'Keep going,' he yelled at her. 'Knock them out of the way.'

But Lucie was pressing the electric button of the window as she braked. Putting her head out, she yelled, 'He's got a gun! Look out.'

With a snarl Rick grabbed her hair and pulled her back. She felt the barrel of the gun cold against her neck. 'Drive, you bitch. *Drive!*'

But Lucie kept her foot on the brake until with an oath he reached across with his foot and kicked hers off the pedal, then pressed down the accelerator. The car shot forward, hit one of the police cars and, being the heavier vehicle, started to push it out of the way, a gap opening before them. Rick gave a shout of triumph and pressed harder on the accelerator, then saw that a policeman had run alongside and pulled open the driver's door. 'Keep away or she gets it,' he screamed out, letting the man see the gun.

Lucie gave a cry of terror but tried to steer the car away from the growing gap. But Rick hit her and pressed on the throttle again, and then they were through, the tearing metal of the car adding its own jarring scream to shatter the night.

Suddenly, just as they were gathering speed, the door on Rick's side was jerked open and someone leapt half on top of him, catching the hand with the gun and pulling it away from her. Then she heard Seton's voice and knew it was him. She turned to help him but he yelled, 'Jump, Lucie. Jump!'

They were struggling together, fighting for control of the gun, of the car.

Petrified with fear for him, she cried, 'No! I can't leave you.'

But Seton shouted frantically, 'Go, my love. *Jump!*'

The car slowed a little as Rick tried to fight Seton off, so with a sob of fear Lucie opened her door, put her arms over her head and let herself fall out. She landed with a thud that took her breath away, and found herself rolling down a slope, bruising her legs and hurting her ankle. But fear for Seton overcame any hurt and she quickly scrambled to her feet and climbed back up the slope, tried to run along the road after the car, but a policeman came up and caught hold of her.

'My husband! He's in the car. Oh, help him, please help him.'

But other men were already running past her, racing after the car. It disappeared round a bend in the road and she began to cry with dread. Then there was a loud noise, a boom like an explosion, she saw a flash and flames through the trees. For a moment every sense seemed to stop, then she heard a scream that was her own and she had pulled herself free and was running down the road.

The car had hit a tree, hit it hard, and burst immediately into flames.

'Seton!' Her terrified cry made them turn towards her. Two policeman barred her way, stepped in front of her so she couldn't see. She pictured Seton inside the car, burning, dying, and struggled to get past, to get him out. But then she heard a shout and saw a policeman helping someone up from where he'd been lying at the side of the road. The man stood and she recognised his shape even in the darkness, even before she saw his face in the light of the flames. They let her go and with a cry of pure joy Lucie ran to throw herself in his arms, to go back where she belonged.

It was many hours later; the day was almost over and it was getting dark. They were at home, the three of them, with nothing, physically, to show for the previous night but a few bruises. Most of the day had been spent at the police station, being interviewed by first one lot of policemen then another, Lucie with her hand in Seton's, holding it very tightly.

He knew everything now, had known most of it before. It seemed that when the police in Manchester had arrested her, they had looked her up on their computer and found out about her past, then passed on the information to the local police, who had in turn talked to Seton on the phone the first day she'd been home.

The computer had, of course, thrown up her connection with Rick, and the police had been looking for him again for some time. They had persuaded

Seton to let them put a tap on the phone while he and she were out with Sam, and that evening he had gone to the pub and met the police there. Even while he'd been talking to them they had picked up Rick's call, had known about the burglary before Lucie had called them. They even knew where it was because they'd put a tracking device in her car. The car that was now a burnt-out wreck and in which Rick had died.

The police had been very kind, considering. They were told they were free to go, that technically Lucie had committed no crime and there would be no charges.

They ate and put Sam to bed; he'd been quite excited when he'd woken that morning to find 'a police lady' waiting to spend the day with him, but had run to them when at last they had got home.

When they were alone, Seton drew her down beside him on the settee. Stroking her hair where it curled on her neck, which was still bruised by Rick's fingers, he said, 'You know, there are some questions I still have to ask you.'

Lucie sighed. 'Yes. You want to know why I didn't tell you, when we first met, that I'd been to prison.'

'That is definitely one of them,' he agreed. 'It came as quite a shock when the police told me.'

'Surely you can guess? I was so ashamed of my past. I made up a story to cover those years and whenever I was asked—when applying for a job, getting to know a friend, that kind of thing—that was the story I told.' She gave a wry laugh. 'It was what I wanted to believe, I suppose. So when you asked me that first evening we spent together, when we had the Chinese meal, I told you too. I didn't expect to see you again, you see.'

'But then I made it clear that I wanted to go on seeing you for the rest of my life and you were in a quandary.'

Lucie nodded. 'I was afraid that I was wrong for you, that I'd let you down.'

'Which you never have,' Seton said loyally.

'How can you possibly say that after the last few months?' Lucie protested. 'I've brought you such misery and wretchedness. I was trying so hard to keep it all from you, to save you from hurt, but everything kept getting worse and worse.'

The fingers that were stroking her hair became still. 'Couldn't you have trusted me? You've been living a lie all these years...'

She turned her head to look at him, her eyes in the lamplight very intense. 'I was always petrified that if you found out I might lose you.'

'Surely you knew that I would never leave you?'

'Oh, yes, I knew you'd stay because you're an honourable man—but there are other things to lose that could have destroyed us. I was afraid of losing your respect, of falling off the pedestal you'd built under me. I was afraid that other people might find out and you'd lose your friends, your parents might turn against me, your colleagues talk about you behind your back. I could see you being thought un-suitable to take important cases, you being pushed out of chambers.' She paused and her eyes grew sad. 'I still can, when all this comes out.'

'It won't,' Seton said strongly. 'Ravena is dead and as far as the police is concerned the case is closed.'

She raised strained, terrified eyes to his. 'He took Sam once; he said that even if I went to the police one of his friends would take Sam away from us.'

Seton put a finger over her lips. 'He didn't have any friends; he was too untrustworthy. You mustn't be afraid of that. It was just an empty threat to make you do what he wanted.'

'Oh.' Lucie looked at him with hope shining in her face. 'Does that mean that Sam will be safe?'

'Quite safe,' he assured her. 'I'm certain of it.'

Balling her hands into fists, Lucie looked away. There was still something that had to be said, an option she had to give him. With great difficulty, she said, 'If—after this, now that you've found out I'm an ex-con, you feel that you'd rather we didn't go on together, that you'd like us to part, I shall—shall quite understand.'

Putting a finger under her chin, Seton tilted her head to look at him. 'I listened to the tape the police made of Ravena's phone call to you. He told you he was going to Spain, that you'd never hear from him again. You could have gone along with that, could have let him do the burglary and said nothing. Been free of him at last. But you called the police. Why did you do that, Lucie?'

She gave a small shrug. 'I knew he was lying. When he ran out of money he would have come back, made me go through it all again. I would never have been free of him. And he kept threatening Sam. I was left with only two choices, and I decided to take a chance, find out where he was going and then stop him so he'd go back to prison.'

'Two choices? What was the other?'

She lowered her eyes. 'To make sure I was out of his reach—permanently.'

'Lucie! No!' Seton's arms went round her and he held her very tight, his face filled with horror. 'How could you even think of doing such a terrible thing?'

'I didn't, not for very long. When I thought of you and Sam... I'm such a coward.'

'No, never that.' He kissed a tear that trickled down her cheek. 'How can you say you're a coward when you tried so hard to protect us, making yourself ill, trying to cope alone?'

Pulling her onto his lap, he encompassed her in his arms, trying to make his strength hers, kissing her forehead, her eyes, her cheeks. 'It's over,' he told her. 'No one will ever know. Our friends, my parents, they thought you were at your aunt's. We can pick up our lives again. You're safe now. You're home, my love. No one will ever hurt you again. I'll take care of you, you know that. Sam and I, we'll always be here to protect you. I love you. I love you more than anything in the world.'

His lips moved to her mouth, so that he couldn't speak any more, but his deepening kiss, the passion that grew out of it, was a greater reassurance than any words.

After a while Seton rose, still holding her in his arms, and carried her towards the stairs. When they were in bed together Lucie gave a great sigh of content and said, 'I feel as if I've been on a very long journey and have come safely home.'

'I know how you feel.'

'I wish I could make it up to you.'

'You can.' Seton whispered in her ear.

Lucie laughed. 'I'll do my best.'

And a few months later, on a frosty night when the moon silvered the trees, she made it up to him in full measure when she gave Seton what he'd asked of her: the daughter that he had so longed for to make their family and their happiness complete.

HARLEQUIN PRESENTS®

Coming in September...

~~Breaking~~ *Making Up*

by
Miranda Lee and
Susan Napier

Two original stories in one unique volume—
"Two for the price of one!"

Meet two irresistible men from
Down Under— one Aussie, one Kiwi.
The time has come for them to settle old scores
and win the women they've always wanted!

Look for ~~*Breaking*~~ *Making Up* (#1907)
in September 1997.

Available wherever Harlequin books are sold.

Take 4 bestselling love stories FREE

Plus get a FREE surprise gift!

Special Limited-time Offer

Mail to Harlequin Reader Service®

3010 Walden Avenue
P.O. Box 1867
Buffalo, N.Y. 14240-1867

YES! Please send me 4 free Harlequin Presents® novels and my free surprise gift. Then send me 6 brand-new novels every month, which I will receive months before they appear in bookstores. Bill me at the low price of $2.90 each plus 25¢ delivery and applicable sales tax, if any*. That's the complete price and a savings of over 10% off the cover prices—quite a bargain! I understand that accepting the books and gift places me under no obligation ever to buy any books. I can always return a shipment and cancel at any time. Even if I never buy another book from Harlequin, the 4 free books and the surprise gift are mine to keep forever.

106 BPA A3UL

Name	(PLEASE PRINT)	
Address	Apt. No.	
City	State	Zip

This offer is limited to one order per household and not valid to present Harlequin Presents® subscribers. *Terms and prices are subject to change without notice. Sales tax applicable in N.Y.

HARLEQUIN WOMEN KNOW ROMANCE WHEN THEY SEE IT.

And they'll see it on **ROMANCE CLASSICS**, the new 24-hour TV channel devoted to romantic movies and original programs like the special **Romantically Speaking-Harlequin® Goes Prime Time**.

Romantically Speaking-Harlequin® Goes Prime Time introduces you to many of your favorite romance authors in a program developed exclusively for Harlequin® readers.

Watch for **Romantically Speaking-Harlequin® Goes Prime Time** beginning in the summer of 1997.

If you're not receiving ROMANCE CLASSICS, call your local cable operator or satellite provider and ask for it today!

Escape to the network of your dreams.

ROMANCE CLASSICS

As Seen on TV!

Free Gift Offer

With a Free Gift proof-of-purchase
from any Harlequin® book, you can receive
a beautiful cubic zirconia pendant.

This stunning marquise-shaped stone is a genuine cubic
zirconia—accented by an 18" gold tone necklace.
(Approximate retail value $19.95)

Send for yours today...
compliments of ❖HARLEQUIN®

To receive your free gift, a cubic zirconia pendant, send us one original proof-of-purchase, photocopies not accepted, from the back of any Harlequin Romance®, Harlequin Presents®, Harlequin Temptation®, Harlequin Superromance®, Harlequin Intrigue®, Harlequin American Romance®, or Harlequin Historicals® title available at your favorite retail outlet, together with the Free Gift Certificate, plus a check or money order for $1.65 U.S./$2.15 CAN. (do not send cash) to cover postage and handling, payable to Harlequin Free Gift Offer. We will send you the specified gift. Allow 6 to 8 weeks for delivery. Offer good until December 31, 1997, or while quantities last. Offer valid in the U.S. and Canada only.

Free Gift Certificate

Name: _____

Address: _____

City: _____ State/Province: _____ Zip/Postal Code: _____

Mail this certificate, one proof-of-purchase and a check or money order for postage and handling to: HARLEQUIN FREE GIFT OFFER 1997. In the U.S.: 3010 Walden Avenue, P.O. Box 9071, Buffalo NY 14269-9057. In Canada: P.O. Box 604, Fort Erie, Ontario L2Z 5X3.

FREE GIFT OFFER   084-KEZ
ONE PROOF-OF-PURCHASE
To collect your fabulous FREE GIFT, a cubic zirconia pendant, you must include this
original proof-of-purchase for each gift with the properly completed Free Gift Certificate.

084-KEZR

Let's Celebrate!

LOVE & LAUGHTER™

invites you to
the party of the season!

Grab your popcorn and be prepared to laugh as we celebrate with **LOVE & LAUGHTER**.

Harlequin's newest series is going Hollywood!

Let us make you laugh with three months of terrific books, authors and romance, plus a chance to win a FREE 15-copy video collection of the best romantic comedies ever made.

For more details look in the back pages of any Love & Laughter title, from July to September, at your favorite retail outlet.

Don't forget the popcorn!

Available wherever
Harlequin books are sold.

 ◆ **HARLEQUIN**®